CW00841371

The Video Game Kids

Martin Smith

For Rob,
aka the Colonel

CHAPTER ONE

An excited hush fell over the television studio.

Everyone waited.

"Three, two, one, action," whispered the producer as the camera's red light came on.

Applause erupted as popular video game influencer Squit bounced into view on the stage.

He bowed to the crowd before settling into one of the two empty chairs.

"Thank you, thank you, thank you all. Welcome to a fascinating episode of Appy Show. Let's not mess around. You know who's here today.

"Please give a warm welcome to Clinton Frogsher, the legendary gamer known as Frogton and, of course, creator of ultimate video challenge – OverPower."

People were already on their feet. Many had been clapping before Squit finished the introduction.

"Frogton! Frogton! Frogton!"

A man, dressed in an expensive black suit and shoes, danced with twinkle toes towards the empty chair opposite Squit.

"Good evening, Squit."

"Good evening, Clinton. Thank you for joining us."

"Not at all, my friend. And please, whenever I talk about games, I like to be known as Frogton as you well know, my good man!"

The crowd burst into another round of applause and chanting. "Frogton! Frogton! Frogton!"

Squit blushed with embarrassment.

"Of course, my apologies."

Frogton smiled a touch. "Do not fret. I am always the world's happiest man, particularly when we are on the eve of the planet's greatest tournament."

Frogton's dark hair had been swept backwards in a trendy hairstyle. He was of average height and build.

He did not seem remarkable. The only clue to his brilliance was the incredible sparkle in his strikingly blue eyes. Yet everyone knew Frogton was a genius.

He turned to the audience and asked with a devilish grin: "Shall we get straight to it?"

They replied as one.

"Yes!"

He looked directly into the camera. The audience was about 150 people, but the world was watching online. The planet stopped when Frogton spoke.

He beamed: "Why waste time? That's my motto. Now convince me properly – do you want to hear about this year's competition?"

"YES," the audience roared, including Squit, who had forgotten he was the interviewer.

Frogton was like this.

He'd hated school and failed any exams.

But Frogton was the best gamer the world had ever seen. Then he went one better – he created the ultimate video game: OverPower.

It was a challenge that no one had beaten.

Frogton was a genius. When he spoke, you listened. It was simple. And today he wanted to talk.

"When I created OverPower 19 years ago it was my proudest achievement.

"It remains the high point – even today.

"This year, OverPower returns on…."

Silence. The event always happened in April, but the actual date moved around.

Not a sound. No one even dared to breathe.

"… April 21."

Whoops of joy filled the packed studio.

The world's greatest tournament was back, another chance for glory.

Squit clapped eagerly. His microphone was now on the floor, forgotten as Frogton spoke.

This was a one-man show.

Frogton held his hands out to calm the crowd. It was not easy.

"The rules remain the same. They are simple.

"Every contestant must be aged 11.

"Schools must submit a team of four players.

"This year's OverPower will begin at precisely 10am.

"Every team must begin at that moment. Any delay will result in immediate disqualification."

Frogton paused. He loved moments like this.

"The prize …" he said slowly, aware this was the part that people desperately wanted to hear.

"… will remain the same as before."

The crowd erupted. Shouting. Cheering. Clapping. Some were hugging.

This time Frogton did not appeal for calm.

Instead, he leapt on to the chair opposite Squit and bellowed towards the crowd.

"Yes! It's true.

"If a team has the talent, ability and determination to beat the ultimate challenge, they will be given a unique position at the world's most significant company – Frog Gaming Industries!

"And their job … will be to play and create the best video games for the rest of their lives."

Working at FGI was the dream for every child

across the planet. Only the brightest minds got that chance.

But a chance to work in the company's incredible video games department? It was a mouth-watering prize.

It had never happened, though. To get in, you had to complete OverPower – the unbeatable game.

Yet the opportunity was there – again.

Frogton smirked.

It was time for the grand finale. These people deserved to know. He cleared his throat.

"This year, the format of OverPower has been tweaked. People have never got close to winning. It was a waste of time and much talent.

"We've learned so much in the 19 years since launch.

"The OverPower experience is a once-in-a-lifetime opportunity. It will not be easy to complete, but it can be done.

"We have never had a winner before, and we want that to change."

CHAPTER TWO

Fozzy Boddy backed away as the angry boys approached, one of them covered in sticky purple goo.

It wasn't his fault.

It had been an accident.

He hadn't meant to spill the drink over the stairs, where it had landed on the school bully.

These things always happened to Fozzy.

Moments earlier, the bottle of squash had slipped out of his grasp.

Desperately he'd tried to grab it, but he was too late, and it plunged down the stairs.

It was no surprise because Fozzy could not catch.

He was useless at all sports.

He'd tried so many times, but his legs and arms didn't listen to his brain.

With curly brown hair and thick glasses, Fozzy was a geek, and he was rather proud of it.

He could win chess matches.

He was a master at building card houses. Maths seemed like the simplest thing in the world. But real life was not like times tables.

Fozzy was constantly one step away from an accident.

People said he would grow out of it.

Yet here he was, 11 years old and still an awkward bumbler.

When a cry of shock exploded from below, Fozzy knew he was in big trouble.

The floor below wasn't far — six steps up, and the gang clocked Fozzy as the culprit straight away.

Leon Dextrose, the meanest kid in the school, had giant bug eyes and arms that should've belonged to a professional wrestler.

And today, his white school shirt was covered in summer fruits drink.

He looked mad.

"Did you do this? I'm soaked – thanks to you being the funny man."

Leon and his gang – Rick, Mick and Gary – surrounded Fozzy, who couldn't get the words out.

"I'm sorry. I didn't mean…."

Leon interrupted, his eyes blazing and cheeks bright red with fury.

"Too late for apologies, Boddy. You've ruined my clothes.

"It's time for you to join your bottle down there."

Fozzy's eyes widened.

He was stocky – his mum often called him barrel boy – but Fozzy wasn't strong. He was no match for them.

Couldn't someone stop this madman?

Where were the teachers?

Before he knew what was happening, they grabbed Fozzy and began to push him over the railings.

CHAPTER THREE

TC sneaked past the group of struggling boys, heading back towards the classroom. She couldn't wait to go to an all-girls school next year.

She was sick of these idiots.

Today they were picking on Fozzy. Tomorrow it would be someone else.

Maybe her, although probably not.

TC did not interest them.

She was small, fragile and painfully shy. They did not notice her most of the time, thankfully. Her long blonde hair covered the hearing aids in both ears and helped her blend in.

She'd been a pupil at East Street Primary for seven years, but it had never got easier like the adults promised it would.

As a result, TC still did not speak in class and never put up her hand to answer a question.

It did not mean she did not know the answers. She almost always did.

But speaking in front of other people terrified her.

Just the mere thought made her feel dizzy and sick at the same time. She hated crowds.

TC risked a look as she edged past them.

Fozzy's head was almost over the railing. The rest of him would soon follow.

One of Fozzy's feet smacked into her back, but she slipped by without making a sound.

Whatever had happened, Fozzy didn't deserve to get thrown down the stairs. Fozz, as TC called him to nobody apart from herself, wouldn't harm a fly.

Except he was the clumsiest person she'd ever met. A gust of wind could blow him over.

They weren't friends. They didn't talk.

But TC liked him more than anyone else in their class. He was a good person.

And that meant something.

Their classroom was at the far end of the corridor. It was precisely 94 steps between Mrs Tomlinson's class and the library.

They were the only places that TC ever went during the school day. Apart from the toilet, if she was desperate.

TC had no friends.

When she started school, she longed to play with the others.

She dreamed of going to birthday parties or having other kids play around her house.

It never happened.

When the doctors decided TC needed a hearing aid, it was too late.

Perhaps the other kids had asked her to play in those early days, and she never heard them.

Possibly they thought she was rude and gave up trying.

She'd never know, although sometimes she did wonder.

Now she could hear perfectly, but still no one asked her to join in or came to sit next to her.

And the birthday parties continued to involve the entire class – except her.

Nothing changed, apart from she could now hear the laughter and arguing every day.

For years it hurt being left out.

Now, she ignored them all.

They didn't know she was ignoring them. But, of course, it was hard to tell when you never spoke anyway.

TC reached the classroom and pushed open the door. Mrs Tomlinson was there, marking a pile of books. The door clicked shut, blocking out the din from the corridor.

The teacher stared sternly at TC over the half-moon spectacles perched on the end of her pointy nose.

"You're a bit early. Lunch still has another," she checked her gold watch with a flourish, "four minutes to run, Thalia-Claire."

TC's cheeks flushed. She despised her full name.

TC was annoyed but did not react.

She had to tell her about Fozzy. He was going to get hurt. She could stop it. She wanted to help.

TC steeled herself. She could do this.

"Well?" Mrs Tomlinson was a kind and generous teacher, but she did not like her lunch hour being disturbed without good reason.

TC's teeth nibbled her bottom lip.

A faint shriek came through the door. It was impossible to tell if it was Fozzy or not.

She wanted to tell the teacher. She had to help Fozz. It was only words. But something inside stopped her.

Fozzy was under attack, and TC couldn't find the courage to help him.

As TC battled herself, the door flung open.

"Miss, come quick. They're going to hurt him badly."

CHAPTER FOUR

A crowd had begun to gather at the bottom of the stairs.

Every pupil stared upward, watching Fozzy dangle over the railing.

Belle Harper heard the commotion and sighed.

Another day, another drama at East Street School.

She pushed her bag into the too-small locker and moved towards the growing crowd.

"What is going on?"

The girl next to her, who was a year younger, shrugged.

"I dunno. Someone got hit by a drinks bottle, they're saying. And apparently, that guy's the one who threw it."

Belle wrinkled her nose and adjusted her dark hair, sitting in a loose ponytail.

It sounded like Fozzy shouting. No way would he throw a bottle – he didn't have a bad bone in him.

Besides, he'd never manage to hit anyone anyway.

There wasn't a teacher nearby and not enough time to look. Somebody was going to get hurt if she didn't act.

Belle never backed down from a challenge. Straight away, she knew exactly who was behind it.

It was always the same bunch.

They'd been in a class for seven years and Leon's gang overstepped the mark every day.

Belle pushed through the crowd towards the stairs, avoiding the sticky juice on the floor.

She stopped next to Sam, watching the incident with a face like thunder.

"Can you catch him?"

Belle asked the question but kept her eyes fixed on Fozzy's struggling legs.

Sam shrugged. He was super strong, like an old tree that barely moves in a storm.

No one messed around with Samuel Burton. He was kind and fair, rarely got into fights. He was so big that no one would dare to threaten him.

Even the bullies hesitated when Sam was around.

"Yeah, I've got him," he replied, lazily rubbing the shaved ginger hair on his neck.

"Thanks, buddy," answered Belle. And she meant it too.

Satisfied Fozzy would not be hurt with Sam there, she pushed through the crowd and leapt up the stairs.

"Let him go," Belle demanded as she reached the top.

"Get lost, Harps. This has got nothing to do with you," Leon sneered.

"No. Stop it now."

Belle's hands curled into fists. She loved sport and was no pushover. She had never been scared of them.

"Belle, help!" Fozzy wailed as he desperately battled the bigger boys.

"Don't worry, Fozzy. We've got you."

"We?"

Leon took a peek over the railing to see Sam standing there, ready to catch his classmate.

"Tell Burton to do one because it doesn't concern him either."

Belle did not answer. Instead, she plunged into a small space between Gary and Rick, grabbed Fozzy's shirt and pulled hard.

Fozzy shrieked, but it caught the others by

surprise.

Belle fell backwards, her hand locked on Fozzy's shirt and hauled him back to safety.

Then strong arms tore her grip away from Fozzy and a knee crashed painfully into her side, making Belle gasp.

Leon pushed her away.

"Beat it, Harps, before I lose my temper."

The bully – still covered in fruit squash – grabbed Fozzy and pushed him towards the barrier again.

Belle was not strong enough to beat them on her own, but she was still smarter.

Ignoring the pain in her side, she fled towards the classroom and, seconds later, crashed through the door without knocking.

Mrs Tomlinson was there, as usual, with Thalia-Claire lurking near the doorway.

Belle was rarely rude but she did not have time.

"Miss, come quick. They're going to hurt him badly."

CHAPTER FIVE

By now, Squit had put the microphone down.

There was no point pretending this was an interview.

It was not.

There were no questions. Squit watched, like the rest of the world, only with a better seat.

Frogton was rarely seen in public. He hardly ever spoke, so people listened when he did.

Everyone in the television studio hung on every word. Millions more followed online.

Frogton marched around the small stage as he talked. Beads of sweat began to form on his smooth forehead.

"For 19 years, The OverPower has bamboozled the brightest. It has flummoxed the fittest.

"It has scared the strongest and terrified the toughest."

Everyone knew this.

People across the world followed OverPower. Last year, half the planet tuned in to watch.

It was a phenomenon.

Three years ago, a Canadian team lasted 57 minutes inside the game.

No one else had gone anywhere near as far. The previous record, posted by an American team, had been 36 minutes.

As ever, Frogton could guess what the audience was thinking. It was one of his biggest strengths.

Being a genius helped with things like that.

"People say the Canadian team were close. They are WRONG.

"They were nowhere near."

Audience members gasped. Was this true?

The media had suggested the Canadian team had been a whisker away from beating OverPower.

Frogton scoffed: "Let me put those silly reports right, once and for all.

"Nobody has ever got past the first stage. It is disappointing but true."

The audience gasped as one.

Frogton smiled.

"Yes, that's right.

"No one has passed the opening phase. Not a single team has been successful in all these years.

"When we built the game, we devised THREE levels. Each level is entirely different, providing a strength, wits, or endurance test.

"And it has been more than a match for children worldwide."

Jaws dropped open.

Eyes widened.

This was unbelievable. After all these years, no one had even completed a third of the tournament.

Pleased with the shocked reaction, Frogton added a new twist.

"Before we find those special kids who deserve a role at FGI, we have a lot more of the game to complete.

"Is it impossible? Absolutely not.

"Is it absurdly hard. Of course!

"I will give one clue. Make of it what you will.

"OverPower challenges everything. Without that, you have nothing."

CHAPTER SIX

"I have been a headteacher for 30 years but I have never witnessed such disgraceful scenes.

"A pupil was being dangled over the stairs? This is shocking."

Beatrice Millman stood in front of the oldest kids in East Street Primary with a face like thunder.

"I am disgusted. Not only with the people involved but those who stood and watched. They are just as guilty.

"As a result, I have no choice but to take drastic action."

The children sitting in front of the headteacher shuffled uncomfortably.

Rarely did Mrs Millman get upset.

She was an excellent head.

Every morning, she stood at the school gates to welcome the pupils and parents with a friendly greeting.

She was someone who loved being a teacher. She knew the name and face of every child in the school.

But today was different.

The cheerful face did not light up with an easy smile. On the contrary, the lips were thinner than ever.

Mrs Millman was mad.

She continued: "This is the last chance.

"We still do not fully know what happened at lunchtime.

"I will ask for one final time: if you saw who was involved, please come forward now.

"This is your final opportunity. You do not want

to keep quiet. Trust me."

Belle squeezed a look at Leon and his cronies.

They were smirking, knowing they'd gotten away with it.

Belle told the teachers what had happened, but no one else had come forward.

Fozzy was too scared and refused to talk about it.

According to Mrs Tomlinson, Sam was too far away to see who was involved, being on the ground floor.

Leon and the rest denied it. It was their word against Belle's.

It happened all the time.

Not a single hand went up. No one dared to speak out.

TC sunk further into her seat.

Silence.

Mrs Millman scanned the faces of the children.

She'd known them for almost seven years and they only had a couple of months before they left.

But they'd overstepped the mark.

"Very well. This gives me no pleasure.

"I have decided that – for the first time in our history – we will not submit a team for OverPower."

"NO!"

Cries echoed around the school hall.

"Miss, you can't do this!"

"This isn't fair!"

"Miss, you're picking on us."

Mrs Millman spoke over the complaints.

"I do not want to hear it. Your behaviour has been disgraceful."

East Street had selected its team for this year's OverPower contest two weeks earlier.

The chosen four were always called East Street Champions.

Ali Waliaz, the school's cleverest pupil, had been the first pick.

Football player Billy Buwst and martial arts expert Rick Palan, one of Leon's gang, were champions too.

The final selection had been Helen Clark, known as 'Clarkie', the fastest runner in the school with an incredible knowledge of television, particularly soap operas.

They were the lucky four that would represent the school at OverPower.

It was a great honour. Now the fight had ruined their dreams.

The bell rang. The school day was over.

Mrs Millman clapped her hands so loudly the sound bounced off the walls.

"You have no one to blame but yourselves.

"I will contact FGI this evening and tell them East Street Primary officially wishes to withdraw from this year's OverPower competition."

CHAPTER SEVEN

"You can't do this, Bea."

Jennifer Tomlinson handed Beatrice Millman a cup of tea in the deserted staff room.

They had been friends for a long time, too many years for either of them to remember.

They knew each other inside out.

The school day had finished. Gradually, the staff drifted away to leave the two of them.

The headteacher replied with a sigh.

"I know, I know. I just wanted a reaction.

"We both know Ricky was part of the awful events, even if there is no way of proving it."

Mrs Tomlinson agreed.

She said calmly: "I wish I'd got there sooner. By the time I'd arrived, Fozzy was in the corner, looking upset.

"There was no sign of anyone trying to throw him over the stairs like Belle said, although I expect she is telling the truth.

"Belle is a good girl."

Mrs Millman looked out at the empty playground. Tears began to fall silently down her cheeks.

"Jen, I have been here for 30 years and I have never felt ashamed of my pupils like I do today. I've never known anything like this."

The words hung in the air.

Mrs Tomlinson waited a moment before pressing on.

"I understand, but we can't punish everyone.

"They only get a single opportunity to do this. Most of them won't even get that.

"One chance. That's it.

"It is not fair, Bea. OverPower means so much to these children.

"We have good kids in our school. They don't deserve to miss out.

"I understand if you want to change the school champions, of course, but they shouldn't all take the blame for the actions of a small minority."

Mrs Millman sipped the lukewarm cup of tea in her hand.

"You are correct, as usual.

"Three of the four champions were there while this nonsense was happening, and they did not try to stop it. They could have stepped forward and been honest.

"Instead, they decided to say nothing. These are not the sort of characters I want to represent our school."

"Fret not. I think I have the answer to sort out this mess," Mrs Tomlinson replied, with a twinkle in her eye.

CHAPTER EIGHT

East Street's record in OverPower was terrible.

The school's longest game in 19 years of competition had been a measly 14 minutes.

They were not alone. The FGI website broadcast every attempt, so it was easy to follow a single team.

Usually, a trip into OverPower did not last long.

Most teams failed to survive for 10 minutes. The average was six.

The UK's longest time had been set 12 years ago. The team – from Bognor Regis – had lasted an incredible 32 minutes.

The US record was four minutes longer. The team, who represented a school in South Carolina, held the world record with a 36-minute stint – until the Canadians topped the lot.

It was the same obstacle that finished most of the teams. The Roller.

It was an enormous block – similar to a giant rolling pin – that raced towards desperate contestants who could not escape.

People accepted the game would soon be finished if you saw The Roller coming.

First, they tried to outrun it. It always caught contestants, even the speediest.

They tried to dodge it, but it was too broad.

Some tried to climb on it. Unfortunately, that did not end well either.

No one escaped The Roller. OverPower was more remarkable than one mere challenge, though. That's why you could never predict what you would be facing.

Every game was different, depending on the choices you made.

Researchers looked endlessly for patterns, determined to beat Frogton's ultimate challenge.

They'd scoured hours and hours of in-game footage, looking for anything that could provide an edge. There had been some wild theories too.

Boffins in the Far East worked out that an anagram of 'The OverPower' was 'Pee Overthrow'.

This discovery caused much excitement. Finally, the scientists had cracked the riddle and told the world, at least so they thought.

Everyone wanted to believe them but it never made much sense.

Months later, the Japanese team lined up full of confidence. Their game began and the world held its breath in anticipation.

The Roller duly arrived and, instead of running, they bravely turned to face the incoming danger.

No one ran. The team did not panic.

Calmly they produced water balloons filled with wee – smuggled into the game – and threw them when The Roller was almost on top of them.

The barmy plan didn't work.

Their game barely lasted three minutes.

The media loved it. One headline screamed "Wee-ly silly!" and another joked: "Wee nearly did it!"

It was another incredible part of OverPower's jaw-dropping technology. People suddenly realised you could take things into the gaming booth – like the water balloons – and OverPower would replicate these items into the game.

The technology was mind-bending.

Soon everyone was planning to take objects to

help them gain an advantage.

But, as a result, FGI banned anyone from taking in anything to help them in the quest.

Now you were only allowed to enter with your clothes – plus health equipment like glasses.

FGI checked everyone. No bags. No equipment.

It was you against the game. And OverPower won every time. As soon as The Roller appeared, it was game over.

The famous Canadian team only survived because The Roller didn't show up until the end.

It had been an epic race. They'd swam whitewater rapids. They managed to see off a swarm of dangerous and strange creatures (a mix of baboons and alligators, called babligators by the media).

The challenge was nearly complete until The Roller appeared and ended the most extraordinary OverPower run the world had seen. Yet hopes were high this year.

The Canadian team had shown OverPower was beatable. And Frogton himself had said the game would be less one-sided this year.

Schools trained their hand-picked champions for months.

Future competitors watched endless reruns of other teams' failures, figuring out what went wrong and how they would have tackled it differently.

There was hope.

For children worldwide, this was the biggest day of their lives. Apart from East Street School, who were not even taking part.

It was April 21. Mrs Tomlinson's class filed into the hall in silence, genuinely miserable after missing out on their only chance to tackle OverPower.

CHAPTER NINE

Beatrice Millman stood in front of the 30 children.

Straight backed and arms folded, she still radiated anger from yesterday's fighting.

Few looked at her. Most stared at the floor. They did not want to meet her gaze.

Next to the headteacher was a table with a small black box on it

A stern-looking Mrs Tomlinson stood on the other side, peering over her spectacles.

Her grey hair was perfect as ever. Mrs Millman pursed her lips and spoke coldly.

"Children. I was appalled yesterday, as you well know. I felt let down by everyone involved in the fighting and those who stood by and did nothing.

"For that reason, I have removed the chosen East Street champions from OverPower."

Silence.

The pupils knew it was coming and now it was official.

They'd blown it.

Ali Waliaz had a face like thunder.

Billy Buwst looked out of the window, refusing to look at anyone.

Rick Palan sat, arms crossed and scowled.

Clarkie wept openly.

Leon Dextrose smirked.

They were the first year in the school's history to fail to participate in OverPower.

Their chance had gone. The school's history books would remember them for all the wrong reasons.

Mrs Millman let the news sink in before she added:

"However, I realise this is your only chance to tackle OverPower.

"It would be wrong for me to deny some of you this opportunity."

A ripple of excitement raced around the room.

The headteacher continued: "Our selected school champions may feel this unfair, but every one of you witnessed the fighting yesterday and none came to find a teacher.

"You stood by and let it happen. It was not the behaviour we expect from the school's chosen four."

Ali Waliaz's hand shot up. Debating was one of her strongest skills.

Mrs Millman, however, was not in the mood for a discussion.

"Hand down, please, Ali. Now is not the time.

"Perhaps if you'd spoken out as someone dangled Pierre over the stairs, we'd be having an entirely different conversation."

Ali's hand dropped. Tears welled in her eyes. Ali was a model pupil and not used to being told off.

Mrs Millman continued: "As no one has owned up or named the culprits from yesterday's disgraceful scenes, I have no choice.

"Every name from Mrs Tomlinson's class has been written on paper and placed inside this box.

"And yes, it does include the four previous champions. So you still have a chance too."

Clarkie's sniffling stopped.

Billy stared at Mrs Millman in shock.

Ali straightened up with tear-filled eyes.

Rick Palan's arms remained crossed, but the scowl disappeared.

They – and the rest of the class – were back in the

game.

The headteacher's left hand rested on the black box, with the children's eyes glued to it.

"The first four names pulled out will be this year's East Street champions. This is the most important lucky dip of your lives."

Gasps came from the children.

Any of them could get the dream shot.

East Street School would tackle OverPower this year, after all.

This was incredible.

"Let's go. Time is against us, Class 6T. We cannot delay any further."

Mrs Millman picked up the box and shook it vigorously.

"Mrs Tomlinson will select the first name."

Without a word, the teacher plunged a hand deep into the box.

A second later, she pulled out a piece of paper and placed it gently on the table.

Mrs Millman put the box down and opened the scrap of paper.

Every child leaned forward, willing the teacher to read their name out.

She raised an eyebrow.

"Well, this is a surprise.

"The first OverPower champion for East Street School is…."

CHAPTER 10

Mrs Millman paused.

Time seemed to stand still.

Children held their breath.

They urged her to speak.

Mrs Millman smiled.

She repeated herself: "The first OverPower champion for East Street School this year is ... Samuel Burton."

Cries of anguish and disappointment filled the room, drowned out by a loud cheer led by Belle.

Blushing, Sam got to his feet.

The others looked at him enviously.

Belle stood too, clapping and whooping with joy.

"Go, Sam!"

By now, she was jumping up and down with excitement. Anyone would think Belle's name had been pulled out of the box, not Sam's.

Sam approached the four empty chairs set out beside Mrs Millman, who indicated for him to take a seat.

"Well done, Mr Burton. A worthy champion in anyone's book."

Sam nodded. He appeared unable to speak.

The din died almost instantly as Mrs Tomlinson's hand delved into the box again to repeat the process.

Mrs Millman scooped up the new fragment of paper.

People crossed their fingers.

Hopes raised.

Everyone waited.

The headteacher said: "The second OverPower

champion for East Street School will be … Pierre Boddy."

More groans and sighs of anguish filled the hall. Desperation turned to despair.

Fozzy's jaw fell open in shock. His real name was hardly ever used by anyone – except his mum and dad. It took a moment for the reality to sink in.

Belle was on her feet again – and this time, the others joined in.

"Yeah! Fozz! You're going to smash it!"

"Fozzy's the man!"

"Foz-zy! Foz-zy! Foz-zy!"

Mrs Millman beckoned Fozzy forward.

"Today, Pierre, please. We're on a rather tight timetable."

The words were sharp but spoken with a smile, coaxing Fozzy towards the champions' seats.

Fozzy began weaving through the kids to get to the front of the hall.

Miraculously he did not fall. By the time he reached Sam, Fozzy was sweating with concentration.

He collapsed into the seat as Mrs Millman opened the next piece of paper to reveal the third champion's name.

Once more, a hush of anticipation fell over the hall.

This time, Mrs Millman frowned.

It did not last long as the headteacher wiped the disappointment from her face.

"The third OverPower champion for East Street School is … Leon Dextrose."

"GET IN!"

Leon raised both arms in celebration.

"Yes, I'm there. The main man of East Street is

going to do the impossible. You know it."

Leon's gang applauded and cheered.

Apart from those four or five voices, the rest of the room was quiet.

Belle shook her head at the injustice. No way was she cheering this champion.

Leon Dextrose swaggered over to the champions' seats, sat down and whispered to Fozzy: "Move over, Fatty."

Belle watched him intently. She knew he'd do something.

And she was right.

When everyone's attention returned to the final choice, the bully elbowed Fozzy painfully in the ribs.

He had plenty of room. There was no need to do it.

He was still fuming with Fozzy over the spilt drink.

Leon Dextrose held grudges. He did not forget, and he did not forgive.

He was that type of person. Poisonous.

Belle felt sick.

Leon was the least deserving of being a champion. He was a nasty bully.

He'd caused yesterday's fight, but he was being rewarded handsomely instead of being punished.

Belle stared at the four kids who should have been the school's champions.

They looked devastated.

Their dreams had disappeared.

Perhaps they should have done more while Fozzy was attacked, but it was still incredibly tough.

It was a raw deal. They did not deserve it.

But that was life. It wasn't always fair.

And the former champions – like Belle and the others – had one final chance to land a place in OverPower.

Mrs Millman held the piece of paper with the fourth champion's name.

You could hear a pin drop.

Some couldn't look.

The tension was unbearable.

Who would it be?

Would one of the original champions be picked?

Would the school's entire line-up be made up of boys? That had never happened before.

This year was different in so many ways.

It was down to chance.

Mrs Millman raised her eyebrows.

This time it was more surprise than anything else.

She said: "The fourth OverPower champion for East Street School is … Thalia-Claire Parmar."

CHAPTER 11

TC's tummy fluttered.

She wrinkled her nose. Had she misheard? It would not be unusual.

The battery in her left ear aid had been wavering since the walk to school earlier.

She'd forgotten to change it. Mrs Millman's words sounded muffled. Had the headteacher said her name? It seemed like it.

TC sat there, unable to decide what to do. Eyes swivelled in her direction. Gasps of dismay filled the room. Something had happened. Did it involve TC or not?

People started to chatter. The school's final OverPower contestant froze. Her mind raced.

TC was desperate to be chosen. She was not crazy. She knew the importance of the draw but it didn't make it less intimidating.

The OverPower was the event. If you were 11, it was the best thing you could do.

People treated you differently, knowing you were an OverPower champion.

It was a chance to prove yourself.

"Come on, Thalia-Claire. We have a schedule to stick to."

She had been chosen. Immediately her stomach began doing gigantic cartwheels. And gravity-defying backflips. Followed by double summersaults.

She was the fourth champion.

TC rose unsteadily to her feet, looking like a newborn gazelle taking its first wobbly steps.

She did not know how she reached the empty

chair at the front or how she did not fall over.

Everything had become a blur.

Her mind kept asking the same questions:

"How is this possible?"

"Why me?"

"What happens now?"

TC missed Leon's look of distaste as she perched on the seat next to him.

And she was too overwhelmed to hear the bully mutter: "You better not mess this up, moron."

Leon had not spoken to her in years. So why would he talk to her now?

Mrs Millman clapped to regain the kids' attention.

"We have our four OverPower champions for the year — an excellent team who will do us proud.

"Mrs Tomlinson says the team from FGI has arrived, and the final preparations are being made to the OverPower gaming booth as I speak.

"Our champions will be briefed on the challenges they can expect and fill in the necessary paperwork."

Mrs Millman checked her watch with a flourish.

"Time is short. Our champions have ... 53 minutes before their test begins.

"I wish them all the best, as I'm sure you all do.

"Now we have to get moving.

"I will ask you all to head over to the library – in an orderly fashion – where, as usual, you can cheer on your classmates on the big screen…."

As the headteacher spoke, TC remained in a daze.

She hadn't noticed the applause for her selection had been less enthusiastic than the others.

Only a handful had applauded. Most were struggling to cope with the disappointment of missing out.

Clarkie was crying again, and she was not the only one.

Even kind-hearted Belle struggled to raise more than a clap.

Almost in silence, the pupils filed out of the hall, heading towards the library.

The OverPower would take place within the hour.

The lucky dip had quashed their dreams for good.

For them, it was over.

Yet, this was merely the beginning for the lucky quartet of lucky classmates.

CHAPTER 12

The champions were shepherded from the hall into a nearby empty classroom by Miss Spate, a grumpy teaching assistant.

Once inside, Miss Spate told them: "Remain here until Mrs Millman arrives with the OverPower officials."

She left without waiting for a reply, slamming the door behind her.

"Look at that," gasped Sam, looking out the window. The others followed his gaze.

Leon shrugged, trying to play it cool.

Fozzy whistled through his teeth.

"Gosh."

There it was. The silver gaming machine gleamed in the courtyard outside the headteacher's office.

The OverPower console looked – to Fozzy, at least – similar to an alien spaceship.

It had four arms – each easily big enough for a person to run around inside – connected to a large dome at the centre. The contraption was enormous and almost filled the courtyard.

It stood locked and unused for 364 days a year in part of the school forbidden to pupils.

It had no power and simply gathered dust.

Then the big day arrived, and the machine was charged and looked as sleek as the day it arrived.

It made dreams and crushed them too.

Dozens of excited children had entered that machine. All emerged, beaten and disappointed.

Fozzy looked at his fellow champions.

Could they beat OverPower?

No. That would be silly. No one had done that.

What about something else?

Something a little more possible.

Could they beat East Street's previous record?

Fozzy looked at his fellow champions. No. Probably not. He would give it a real good go, though.

His feet might not always listen to him, but he would give 100 per cent, like always.

It wouldn't be enough, he knew. Yet it was all he had to give.

Fozzy watched Leon check his trendy side-parting before turning away from the OverPower console.

With a steely gaze, Leon eyeballed the others.

As the ice-cold stare fell upon him, Fozzy felt a shiver of dread.

Leon sneered: "Let's quit messing around. This is the worst OverPower team in the school's history."

He shook his head.

"No, scrap that. This is the worst OverPower team in the history of the world."

Fozzy hated confrontation.

He did not argue with anyone – apart from his brother Topper – but he wanted to tell Leon to shut up and rise heroically to the challenge.

Yet Leon was right.

He was hopeless at everything. What chance did he have? TC was brainy. Sam was strong. Leon was great at sports.

As he offered nothing except clumsiness, Fozzy opted to stay quiet.

Leon continued: "You … morons," he pointed directly at Fozzy and TC, "had better stay out of our way.

"I'm not getting embarrassed because the school somehow picked you.

"If I were you, I'd be too ashamed to take up space in this team. You two are a waste of time."

TC stared back.

Fozzy's cheeks flushed with shame.

Desperately he racked his mind to say something in response. Anything.

But it was Sam who answered.

"Perhaps, Leon, old fella, you had better stay out of our way."

Arms crossed, the bigger boy positioned himself behind Fozzy and TC.

"We're a team here. You're the one who is in danger of becoming an embarrassment."

Leon's hands curled into fists.

He eyeballed Sam, who looked utterly unbothered.

"Watch your mouth, Burton."

Leon was powerful – a mixture of football and motocross had made him tough and wiry.

But Sam towered over him.

It was no contest. And he simply smiled in response, making Leon madder than ever.

He considered saying something else for a moment, but Fozzy could see the bully having second thoughts.

Very few people fancied their chances against ginger giant Sam Burton.

Instead, Leon tried to act casual.

"Fine. You three stick together. Whatever. I don't care. They'll all see. I don't need you. I'm going into this game with no fear. It doesn't scare me. OverPower should be frightened of me."

CHAPTER 13

Mrs Millman beamed with pleasure as she stood before the school's champions.

It was nearly time. Perched a fraction behind Mrs Millman was a man sporting a huge grin. He was thin like a marathon runner with short dark hair and long clipped sideburns.

"East Street champions. Please meet Benjamin Guffain. He is our FGI representative for OverPower this year."

Sam guessed the man was in his early 20s. No one older than 30 worked for FGI. Everyone knew that.

He wore spectacles that reminded Sam of a teacher, but he was nothing like that when he spoke.

"Yo, yo, yo. Call me Benjy. The champs are in the house! Boys and girls, hold tight because it will be a wild ride!"

Sam wanted to laugh. He didn't know if this guy was taking the mickey or not.

He heard Leon groan but ignored him. If Benjy was disappointed by the reaction, he did not show it. Instead, the game official seemed to get more excited with every word.

"Champions, we have … precisely," he paused to check a state-of-the-art watch on his bony wrist, "… 31 minutes until OverPower 19 kicks off.

"The moment is nearly here.

"It's going to be … phantasmagorical."

Sam frowned. He'd never heard of such a word. Phantasmerwatchacallit?

Fozzy was grinning almost uncontrollably.

TC's eyes glimmered with excitement too.

They got it. Feeling left out of the joke, Sam shifted uncomfortably.

He asked: "What happens now?"

Benjy flashed a winning smile. His favourite part of the day was coming up.

He produced a small orange box with a flourish, which glowed even in the morning light.

The Finger Finder.

The devices were legendary. They were the most precious items of technology in existence.

FGI created them and did not allow anyone else to know how they worked.

Presidents begged. Prime Ministers pleaded. Governments were desperate to get hold of these incredible machines.

Nothing worked. FGI refused to give them to anyone because Finger Finders had been designed for OverPower – and nothing else.

Contestants placed a finger into the machine and allowed the high-tech device to read their fingerprints.

Yet that was not all. The Finger Finder would uncover everything about you.

Naturally, it confirmed your name, age and address.

But it did far more than that.

It could tell:

What you have for dinner every Saturday night.

The number of times you'd lied in your life.

Whether you could swim.

What was your favourite pizza topping.

Why you never did like broccoli.

The Finger Finder uncovered every secret.

This ensured there was no cheating.

You got one chance – and this small box made

sure the competition was entirely fair.

The Finger Finder confirmed the person matched the name provided by the school.

It was a truth-seeker, as FGI described it.

All the contestants stared, transfixed.

Benjy smiled.

"No time to waste, East Street. This is the Finger Finder. It's straightforward and does not hurt at all.

"I will come round to each of you. Place the middle finger of your right hand into the device.

"As you can see, it is currently orange. If everything is correct, the device will turn green. If there is a problem, it will flash red.

"Relax. I've never seen it turn red. Of course, it happened a fair bit when we launched, but these days everyone understands there's no way to cheat the system."

Benjy thrust the Finger Finder in Sam's direction.

When Sam looked dubiously at the small device, Benjy reassured him.

"It takes seconds. It's painless."

Sam nodded. His finger went inside.

It felt like he was stroking a car bonnet, which was neither hot nor cold.

It felt like metal. And nothing else.

Green. Sam breathed a sigh of relief.

"Told you! Nothing to be worried about," exclaimed Benjy, who was already moving down the line as the machine turned back to orange.

TC's finger was ready.

Moments later the result came in: green.

TC smiled and received hearty congratulations from Benjy. Sam patted her on the back.

He'd never seen TC smile before. It made her look

completely different.

Sam realised he barely knew TC even though they'd been in the same class for years.

Benjy moved on. Fozzy shook with fear as his right hand slid into the machine.

"Er, Mr Boddy. One finger please, not an entire hand," Benjy said sternly.

"Oh, sorry!"

Embarrassed, Fozzy removed his hand and carefully did as Benjy requested.

Moments later, the device turned green.

"Get in!"

Sam thought Fozzy might cry with happiness.

In a few minutes, his dream would become a reality.

Benjy moved to the last stop on the line and bellowed a hearty greeting.

"Hello. You must be Leon, my good man."

Leon did not reply. He had a disgusted look, pretending he would prefer to be anywhere else.

Benjy did not react and merely thrust the machine in Leon's direction.

With a scowl, Leon shoved his entire hand into the Finger Finder.

"No! One finger only!"

For the first time, Benjy seemed ruffled.

"Oh dear, I'm so sorry," replied Leon. However, he didn't sound sorry in the slightest.

Unlike Fozzy, Leon did not remove his hand carefully. He yanked it viciously.

As he pulled, the Finger Finder slipped from Benjy's grip and spun across the room.

It crashed in the far corner with a sickening thud.

CHAPTER 14

TC's eyes widened in horror as the Finger Finder flew into the air.

Everything happened in slow motion. The room, full of excitement moments before, fell into a deathly hush as they watched the precious device spin away.

Bang! The Finger Finder smashed to the floor.

Leon had broken it, TC guessed, even though tables and chairs obscured her view.

She could not believe what was happening.

Leon threw his arms up in the air.

"Woah. What did you let go for, man?"

He glared at Benjy, trying to blame the older man for the incident.

TC knew that wasn't the case. She'd seen what happened and was sure Leon had done it on purpose.

There was no reason for it. TC could not understand Leon's thinking, but when did she ever?

This was not right. TC wanted to say Leon had tried to break the machine on purpose.

But, as usual, nothing came out.

It was a repeat of yesterday – when TC had failed to tell Mrs Tomlinson about the fight.

TC longed to shout at the top of her lungs.

At home, her parents couldn't stop her from talking. She was a whirlwind of noise

Yet, whenever she stepped outside the house, something changed. She became anxious and nervous – and she would not talk until she returned home.

TC had nearly finished her time at East Street, and she'd barely managed to utter a single word there.

Today was no different. Feeling hopeless, TC

watched Benjy. The room was silent.

The FGI official stood still like a statue for a second, unsure what to do. And then he laughed.

The noise moved through his body before exploding out of his bearded mouth. It broke the spell.

"Apologies, young man. Silly me. I have always been a butterfingers. Now, let me get the device, and we'll do it properly."

Benjy moved towards the Finger Finder as he replied.

Leon folded his arms defensively.

"You can't. It's broken. We don't have time."

Benjy snorted: "Leon, we always have time! And this machine is not broken, far from it. They have survived far, far worse than a simple accident, my dear chap."

Benjy had reached the machine and scooped it up with barely a second glance.

They did not believe him. Leon must have broken the Finger Finder.

But Benjy did not even check it. Instead, he wiped it down and returned to the front of the room.

Once more, he held out the device.

"See? It seems in good health. Do you think we'd create a truth machine that was breakable?"

Leon seemed angry. He glared at the machine, then Benjy and then the machine again.

Finally, he thrust his finger forward with a sigh.

"Excellent. I told you…."

Benjy's excited voice tailed off.

The machine had turned colour. It was red.

CHAPTER 15

"Children. I am sorry for calling you back into the hall again. Unfortunately, OverPower is nearly upon us, and we have a major problem."

Mrs Millman spoke in a rush, aware time was running short. Every second counted.

"I will be honest. I made a mistake. Leon Dextrose cannot participate in the tournament because he is only 10."

Several gasped.

Others let out yelps of excitement.

There was still one place up for grabs.

Nine minutes to go.

The headteacher continued: "As you know, we always ensure our champions are 11 years old as the competition rules state.

"However, due to the hasty rearrangements, I forgot to apply the same checks – and accidentally included everybody.

"Mr Dextrose did not meet the criteria. Instead, he tried to fool the system, which would never happen."

"Now, I will ask everyone who is 10 to please move to the right side of the hall."

Six people moved to sit with a scowling Leon.

"Thank you for your honesty. This mess is entirely my fault, and I apologise," Mrs Millman said as the class divided.

Mrs Tomlinson picked the names of the underage players out of the list and cast them aside.

"Due to our oversight, Mr Dextrose was given a champion's slot. He did not tell us he was underage. He thought he could cheat the system. It was incredibly foolish and naive.

"The Finger Finder cannot be tricked."

Leon was muttering under his breath. He looked mad.

Mrs Millman did not care.

The boy had wasted valuable time and energy.

Between her mistake and Leon's dishonesty, East Street was perilously close to failing to meet the deadline for this year's OverPower.

Benjy hovered beside her.

"Eight minutes. We need to move," he whispered.

Mrs Millman glanced in Mrs Tomlinson's direction, working feverishly on creating the new draw.

Her friend looked back and nodded. They were ready to go again.

"As a result of today's events, we still have one available slot for a school champion."

She looked at the cluster of faces sitting bright-eyed in front of her.

They warmed her heart.

Such enthusiasm.

Mrs Millman smiled.

"The fourth and final champion for East Street Primary for this year will be…."

Seven minutes left.

Excited faces stared at her.

This was it.

The last chance.

An unexpected bonus.

One of them was going into OverPower.

Mrs Tomlinson passed a scrap of paper over.

Mrs Millman unfurled the winning ticket, cleared her throat and announced: "… Belle Harper."

CHAPTER 16

The Finger Finder flashed green.

Belle was now officially an East Street champion.

They were a team.

Four minutes remained.

The champions stood in the small courtyard as the OverPower machine whirred gently beside them.

Mrs Millman checked her watch.

The school always had OverPower champions briefed and in position at least ten minutes before starting.

Today there was no time, although Benjy appeared relaxed.

He spoke clearly to the children in front of him.

"Champions. We are here.

"Your time has arrived.

"My usual briefing takes ten minutes, and then we have questions.

"Today there is not enough time."

Belle and Sam shared a look of concern.

Benjy did not see it. Instead, he continued: "As you can see, there are four gaming sections on this machine — one for each of you.

"The games console is different to anything you have ever played. When it begins, you become part of the game.

"When you step inside, there will be a sensor headband on a wall hook. Put it around your head and that's it. You're ready.

"You are the game. It is like no other gaming experience. Hence the reason it is so special."

Fozzy interrupted: "So we're attached to one

sensor? Eh? How does that even work?"

Three minutes.

Benjy held up a hand.

"No time to explain. It is all you need. The mind is more powerful than anyone realised – until Clinton Frogsher ripped up the gaming rulebook.

"Step into the booth. The gaming experience is like real life. You do not need to do anything.

"When the contest begins, you become the game. Your appearance and skills may be different. Who knows? I have no idea what's facing you.

"Remember to work as a team.

"Many have failed, but one day someone will beat the game. Why not you?"

The children look stunned. They did not reply.

"One more thing.

"What's your team's name?"

Silence.

Today had been anything but straightforward and, in a rush, they'd forgotten to choose a name.

"Er," replied Belle, biting her lower lip.

Her mind went blank.

She looked at the others. They looked equally lost.

Benjy did not look concerned.

"Right, no problem."

Belle wondered if every FGI worker was like Benjy. Briefly, she wondered what had to happen for him to get upset.

He was a cool cat.

And the lack of a name did not ruffle him.

"Each team's name has to be four words long."

Belle already knew that.

Last year, the school team had been called 'Easy for East Street', which looked pretty silly after their almost immediate elimination.

Four words.

And four champions.

Belle spoke in a rush.

"Right, we need a name. It's four words, and there are four of us, so one word each. Pick the first word you think of, right?"

She did not wait for a reaction.

"Sam, you're at the far end. You start."

"The."

"Cool. Fozzy, you're next."

"Hmm. I want to say 'video game' but I know that's two words. Unless...."

He looked at TC, who stood between him and Belle.

Belle understood.

It was probably the simplest way to do it.

"TC, if Fozzy picks 'video', would you be happy to have 'game' as your choice?"

TC nodded with a relieved smile.

They all looked at Belle.

Her mind raced.

The Video Game ... what?

"First thing that comes into your mind, you said," a small voice whispered in the back of Belle's mind.

She could only think of one word. It was not original or cool, but nothing else was coming.

"Kids."

Benjy did not react. He was already scribbling the team's name down on to his tablet.

"The Video Game Kids. That's an interesting one."

Belle flushed. Benjy was being polite. The was only interesting because it was so lame.

They knew it sounded terrible.

Others would be laughing when it flashed up on the screens.

Still, it was what it was.

They could not change it now.

Two minutes to go.

Benjy clapped.

"The Finger Finder automatically allocated you a booth. Find the one with your name on the digital display.

"Push your thumb to the outdoor keypad and the door will slide open. Step inside and press your thumb to the indoor keypad to close the door.

"The head sensor will be in the centre of the room. Put it around your head and fasten it tight.

"Each section will be fully lit until a few seconds before the game begins. Then it will go dark.

"DO NOT PANIC.

"It is the machine linking with the central computer at FGI headquarters.

"Once the connection is secure, the screen will display a countdown until the start."

Sam pulled a face.

"And what then?"

There were 60 seconds to go.

Benjy smiled and gestured for the kids to find the correct gaming sections.

He replied dramatically: "And then it's your chance to make history."

CHAPTER 17

They scrambled to find the section with their name marked next to it.

Fozzy, as usual, was last. The sensor pad did not recognise his thumb. Three doors clicked open and then shut. Fozzy's stomach tightened. He was trailing the others already, even TC.

"Wipe your thumb, Mr Boddy, and try again."

Benjy gave a small reassuring pat on Fozzy's shoulder. "It happens all the time. Relax."

He was right. Fozzy brushed the sensor, and the door opened for the first time this year.

He stepped into the compartment, with light coming from a small tower in the centre of the room.

On top of the tower stood the sensor that Benjy had spoken about earlier.

"Good luck," said Benjy as the door closed with a hiss, leaving Fozzy alone.

The gaming station was larger than it looked from the outside.

Each wall was a giant screen from top to bottom.

And the floor was a screen too.

At the moment, everything was black.

Fozzy removed the sensor headset from the tower and placed it carefully upon his head. There were no wires or cables.

It was too big, but the sensor realised this and automatically adjusted it to fit Fozzy's head.

Fozzy could feel the device tighten so it would not come loose. It was incredible.

"Wow, that is some serious tech," thought Fozzy, "it's so clever, it's almost scary."

The tower that had held the sensor in the middle of the room sunk into the floor, leaving Fozzy alone with the giant screens.

"This is sick," said Fozzy.

A single word flashed up on the screen.

Welcome

Fozzy's heart was beating like a drum. Both hands were sweating. He needed a drink. His throat felt dry and scratchy.

"I can do this," Fozzy said aloud.

He knew soon he'd be back with the others.

And he was alone in a room where nothing could hurt him. But that didn't stop him from feeling nervous. Or scared. Or terrified.

What had Leon said that had stuck in Fozzy's mind earlier?

"No fear." Yes, that was it.

Fozzy mouthed the words repeatedly as he looked at the seven-letter word in front of him.

No fear. The 'welcome' disappeared into the bright blue nothingness.

It was replaced by the number 10. As Fozzy watched, the number changed to nine. Then eight. It's the countdown, he realised.

No fear. Fozzy thought he might be sick. This was it. The game was going to begin.

Five. Four.

No fear.

Three. Two.

No fear.

One. Go.

The world plunged into darkness.

CHAPTER 18

Sam could not see a thing. It was pitch black.

He was unsure how long he'd been waiting.

It seemed like forever. Darkness was everywhere.

Was this part of the game? Sam called out timidly. "Belle? Fozzy? TC?"

No answer. The sensor gripped his head but was not uncomfortable.

It was the only thing he could see or feel. Even the air was still. The darkness made him feel wobbly. Perhaps it was nerves.

Sam took a deep breath to try to calm down.

And then another. It worked a little.

Benjy, after all, had told them this would happen.

Before him, giant white letters emerged into view.

Welcome to OverPower 19

Sam forgot about deep breathing. This was it.

The games console flashed brightly and, in the blink of an eye, Sam was standing on a road with lush grass verges on either side.

The road was concrete and as straight as an arrow. You could not see the end.

There were no vehicles, trees or anything noticeable around him: only the green grass and the endless road ploughing through the middle of it.

Unseen birds chirped noisily. They were the only sound he could hear.

Sam checked his clothes – he was still wearing his school uniform. There were no fancy costumes. OverPower had given out team kits to contestants in other years, but not this time.

East Street Primary's red jumper and white shirt uniform would be part of their OverPower experience.

And there was nothing he could do about it.

"Hey!"

Belle, Fozzy and TC approached him, their faces full of wonder. They looked the same as they had two minutes earlier.

Sam guessed – correctly – his appearance was unaltered too.

"Ready?"

"Yes," Belle beamed.

"Guess so," replied Fozzy, who was fidgeting as usual.

TC nodded eagerly. Sam smiled. He felt better with the others beside him.

"Great. Not sure what we do now though?"

"Shall we read the sign?"

Belle pointed to Sam's left.

Sam blushed. He'd spawned almost on top of the small signpost but somehow missed it.

Feeling foolish, Sam read the words etched into the wooden cross.

Round One
The Ultimate Challenge

They could only hear the birds. There was no other sound. The sun was shining. Lush grass was all around.

A perfect picture. No hint of danger.

But they knew 'The Ultimate Challenge' would soon be here.

Whatever it was, it did not sound good.

OverPower never started slowly.

There was no time to waste.

"Move!"

Sam roared as he realised the game had started, and they were standing around pointlessly.

The road looked the same in either direction.

He did not discuss which way they should go. Instead, he guessed, went left and shot off at top speed.

The others followed.

From the footsteps, Sam could tell Belle and TC were close behind.

Fozzy was further back, trying to keep up.

Sam's heart was beating like a drum again. It was not the exercise. He could run like this for ages.

It was fear.

Sam – and the others – knew something was coming.

They had seen the road before.

It was not an easy challenge.

You started moving, and OverPower would give you a chance. You thought you could win. Hope flourished.

Then they came.

OverPower waited until you began to believe before crushing those dreams brutally.

They had to get as far down the road as possible before the challenge truly began.

It would not be long.

They ran and ran.

After ten minutes, the pace began to slow.

Fozzy was now almost 50 metres behind the others.

Sam's legs were getting heavier. The others were struggling too.

How could that be?

They were in a video game.

There shouldn't be tiredness.

But OverPower was not like other video games. In here, there was no boundary between the game and real life.

Fozzy was grumbling.

They would have to stop and take a breather.

Sam skidded to a halt and immediately realised he couldn't hear the invisible birds anymore.

Apart from their heavy breathing and Fozzy's chuntering, the place was quiet.

Sam shuddered.

He'd watched enough OverPower to know their first challenge was about to be unleashed.

Belle and TC caught him up while a red-faced Fozzy half ran and half walked to catch up.

Fozzy opened his mouth to say something to the others, who were staring at him.

And, as he did, a terrible sound pierced the air.

Immediately, each of them knew what the first challenge was.

Wolves.

The pack was coming.

CHAPTER 19

"RUN!"

Belle screamed the unnecessary warning as the second howl began, closely followed by a third.

Sam and TC had already taken off, but Belle could not leave Fozzy. He could not move quickly enough.

"Come on, Fozz. Keep coming. You've got this."

Fozzy replied: "Leave me. I can't go on."

But Belle would never allow that.

All of them had been chosen as champions today. They weren't going to give up at the first sign of trouble.

They'd yearned for this chance and could survive anything OverPower threw at them.

Belle was sure of that.

She also knew the best way of achieving the impossible was by sticking together.

Another howl, louder this time.

Belle scanned the horizon. Nothing.

She turned back to Fozzy.

"No, we won't leave you, Pierre. This is a team game. And you – my friend – are an important part of our team."

Fozzy looked startled. No one ever wanted him on their team. And only adults used his first name.

But today was different – on both counts.

He caught up with Belle but, instead of stopping, Fozzy kept going. Then, arms and legs pumping with effort, he raced after Sam and TC.

"Yes, Pierre. You've got this, buddy."

Belle let him move ahead of her and rechecked the horizon. Still no sign.

The howls were continuous now. It sounded like an army marching in their direction.

Wolves' cries filled Belle's brain.

Fozzy. She concentrated on her friend and tried to push the howls away.

He was running flat out, but it wouldn't be enough.

They were moving too slowly.

Perhaps Sam and TC could get away, although Belle did not believe they could.

It was all or nothing.

Ahead, the road began to curve dramatically to the right.

Sam and TC were no longer running.

Why had they stopped? Were they crazy?

Belle had no idea what they were doing. So instead, she kept encouraging Fozzy to keep moving.

Any moment, the chasing pack would come into sight.

Belle accelerated and pulled alongside Fozzy.

She pleaded with him. "Come on, Fozz. Keep going. You've got this."

He did not reply. He could not waste the energy.

Belle checked behind them one more time.

Still clear. Where were they?

Belle looked forward again, doubt filling her mind. They were rapidly catching Sam and TC.

She could now see why they'd come to a halt – it was another wooden noticeboard.

Belle turned to recheck their tail and her stomach lurched. She could see a small black dot in the far distance. A second later, it became three. Then five.

The wolves were here.

Finally they reached Sam and TC, who remained

motionless.

"Why are you two waiting? We're wasting time!"

Belle screeched at the pair as a half-exhausted Fozzy joined them too.

This sign was even more straightforward than the first. It had an arrow pointing towards the road as it curved up to the right.

It said: "Escape this way."

Belle now knew why the road turned right: a vast chasm stood ahead of them.

There was no way across. It was too far to jump, at least the length of two double-decker buses.

There was no bridge. They could not cross it. The Video Game Kids had to follow the sign.

"It doesn't seem right, does it?"

Fozzy raised an eyebrow.

"Why?" Sam asked, looking anxiously behind them. TC had already begun to creep along the road, eager to start running again.

But Fozzy did not seem too concerned about the threat of the fast-approaching enemy.

He scratched his hair.

"This sign is … odd. It makes no sense. OverPower never helps anyone. Why is it helping us?

Fozzy frowned, deep in thought.

Belle checked over her shoulder.

The wolves had closed the gap by half. They would be here in 30 seconds, a minute at the most.

And then it would be game over.

She shouted: "We're wasting time. Let's go!"

TC did not need any further invitation.

Belle and Sam followed. There was the only road ahead.

The wolves would soon be upon them, but they

had to try.

After 30 metres, they heard a voice shout behind them.

Eyes wide open, Fozzy waved his arms frantically: "No. Wait. Don't you get it?"

TC was already out of earshot.

Sam kept going too.

Only Belle turned back.

"What?"

Fozzy moved closer to the edge.

The wolves were now only 350 metres away. Belle could hear their snarls.

"The Ultimate Challenge? How did I not realise it until now?

"No fear. Leon was right."

Belle pulled a face.

Leon?

Has she heard correctly? That weasel bully-boy had never been right in his life.

Had Fozzy lost his mind?

The wolves were 250 metres now and closing fast.

She was desperate to flee.

She wanted to tell Fozzy to stop being an idiot.

But there was no time.

Fozzy looked at her.

"Trust me, Belle."

Then he jumped into the ravine and was immediately swallowed by the darkness.

CHAPTER 20

Gasps echoed around the East Street library as events unfolded on the big screen.

Against all the odds, their classmates had so far survived OverPower.

They'd been lucky, of course.

Most teams' first challenge was The Roller and that was that.

But their team faced the wolves' challenge. Not easy, but not a hopeless task either.

Moments earlier, there'd been a smattering of nervous cheers as the team reached the ravine intact.

They only needed to keep going for another 120 seconds and they would be East Street School's longest surviving champions.

True, beating 11 measly minutes was not the most remarkable success – but it was something.

Then, for some inexplicable reason, the team stopped. Nerves filled the room.

"Run," someone shouted.

"Get moving!"

"They're getting too close."

Soon everyone was screaming at the champions as the wolves steadily closed the gap.

TC began to run and the audience applauded wildly.

Even though the champions couldn't hear, their classmates still urged the others to follow.

By now, the wolves were perilously close.

Fozzy was talking excitedly to the group, claiming Leon had been right.

Leon did not know what Fozzy was talking about

but pretended he did.

The bully sat there smugly as the others stared at him in awe.

Still upset about missing out as one of the school's champions, Rick gave Leon an evil look.

He asked Leon directly: "Fozzy said you were right? So, what have you got to do with this?"

Leon lied: "I helped them. I knew I was going to get found out, so I helped them as much as possible."

Rick did not believe him.

He was sick of Leon. Rick regretted being part of his stupid gang – a lesson he'd learned the hard way.

He turned to concentrate on the events unfolding on the big screen.

Leon spoke so the entire room could hear: "Fozzy needed guidance. I was happy to help. Good to see he listens to people who know."

No one listened. OverPower was the only thing on their minds, not Leon's blatant fibbing.

Then, Fozzy decided to throw himself off the cliff edge out of nowhere.

Everyone watched in horror. No one could quite believe what had happened. Leon didn't look so smug now. What was Fozzy thinking? Why would he do that?

This team were close to creating history.

They may not have escaped the wolves but quitting was not an option.

This was their chance. The only time they'd ever play OverPower. What a waste.

They watched Belle scream and run to the cliff edge.

"Move, Belle!"

Clarkie, eyes still red from crying, bellowed at the

screen. Others shouted useless warnings at the television too.

Then, to everyone's amazement, Belle leapt off the cliff too.

More choking sounds from the crowd. It could not be happening. Fozzy jumping was one thing, but Belle? She was the most sensible person in the class.

Belle never did anything crazy. Now she was gone.

Mrs Tomlinson's heart sank. It was a disaster.

They had been so close but had thrown it away in a couple of crazy seconds.

Yet she could not show that disappointment to the children.

"Come on, East Streeters! Cheer on your remaining two champions! They can still make history."

A roar of support went around the confines of the library. Sam and TC were still in the game.

If they started moving now, they could still survive for long enough to become East Street's best-ever players.

But they stood still, peering over the edge.

The wolves had changed course and were now headed straight for the survivors.

"RUN!"

Mrs Millman yelled at the top of her voice.

Of course, they did not hear her.

Instead, Sam and TC moved closer together.

They held hands. The wolves were almost upon them. But they jumped too before the alpha wolf could sink his teeth into Sam's arm and finish the game.

And the television screen went black amid wails of despair and frustration.

CHAPTER 21

Fozzy crashed on to a strange surface, which felt similar to a trampoline floor with a little less spring.

He bounced several times before rolling forward and staggered to his feet, using a slimy rock as support.

Fozzy tried to calm himself.

"It's only a game. It's only a game, only a game," he chuntered.

It did not feel like a game. It felt real, especially down here in the pitch black.

Fozzy lifted a hand but could not see it.

The darkness did not matter for now.

He'd survived the fall, and his game was not over. He checked his body. Everything seemed to be working.

Had he done the right thing? Was he supposed to be down here?

Time would tell.

Deep inside, Fozzy knew his logic was correct.

Far above, a slither of blue sky could be seen.

As he stared upwards, a black dot appeared for a split second against the blue before disappearing again.

"Arrgggghhhh!"

Belle.

Fozzy would know that voice anywhere.

She'd jumped too.

He couldn't believe it.

People never listened to him.

They put up with his bad jokes and dinosaur facts. Rarely did they pay him attention or listen to his opinion.

But Belle was different.

She listened. She cared.

She was that kind of person.

And now she was falling towards him, Fozzy realised in horror, a split second too late.

Belle missed her teammate by a few centimetres, but the springy floor flung her straight back into the air before crashing into Fozzy's stomach.

"Ooohh!" Fozzy cried out as the pair collided.

"Fozzy? Is that you?"

"Yes," groaned Fozzy as he clambered to his feet again. Luckily, his eyes were becoming used to the gloom, making the task easier.

He helped Belle up.

"Oh, Fozzy. I can't believe you found me so quickly. Thank you. Did you try to catch me?"

High above them, the wolves howled with frustration.

Belle was unaware her fall had wiped out Fozzy. He began to tell her but stopped.

Further up the ravine, they heard the unmistakable sounds of more players plunging off the cliff.

Sam. TC.

The pair had been further along the track on the cliff-top than Fozzy and Belle.

As a result, they had jumped at a different point.

Now Fozzy and Belle had to find them.

"Sam! TC!" Belle shouted hopefully, but it was pointless.

The wolves' cries drowned out any words.

Fozzy gritted his teeth and ignored the ache in his stomach. After all, OverPower was a video game, so they could not be hurt.

Belle's crash landing was nothing.

They had bigger things to worry about right now.

"Follow me," Fozzy said.

Slowly the friends stumbled along the dark passageway, heading in the direction of where Sam and TC leapt.

"Why did you jump Fozzy?"

Still, the wolves' cries echoed at the foot of the canyon.

Despite the sound, Fozzy heard the question.

He'd been waiting for it.

But before he could reply, giant letters emerged in front of them both – hovering in mid-air.

The words shone brightly, easy to read in the dim light.

Round Two
Punishment

Against all the odds, The Video Game Kids had survived the opening round.

CHAPTER 22

"Woah. Get in." Sam's fist pumped in celebration.

TC gasped. Had they reached Round Two? How was that possible? They'd made it further than any other team in East Street's history.

They exchanged a look of excitement, even though they could not see each other's faces due to the light.

As the letters faded away, Sam realised the wolves had stopped howling. They were gone, beaten.

Without the wailing, the sound of Belle's voice reached their ears.

"Where are you guys?"

Sam smiled. He'd told TC the others would look for them, so all they needed to do was stay put.

And he'd been right.

Belle would never go on without them. She would rather quit the game than leave one of the team behind.

Two figures emerged from the gloom.

"Sam? TC?"

"We're right here, guys," replied Sam with a grin that no one could see. "Welcome to Round Two!"

"Hell, yeah!" Belle could not contain her excitement. "And it's all thanks to Fozzy!"

The team reunited with a round of fist bumps and back slaps. Sam could not hide his relief. They could only do this as a team by working together.

"Fozzy, you haven't answered me yet. Are you going to tell us all?"

Sam knew precisely why Belle was pestering Fozzy. He wanted to know the same thing too.

"Yeah, Fozz. That was crazy back there. Whatever

made you do it? Of course, I'm glad you did, but it still blows my mind."

Fozzy hopped from one foot to the other. He hated the spotlight.

"Well, er, um…." Fozzy spluttered, looking like he'd rather be anywhere else.

TC tugged at Belle's jumper anxiously. Belle pulled her arm away.

"No, TC. We need to hear this," answered Belle gently but firmly, turning to Fozzy, "you said something about Leon?"

It gave Fozzy a starting point.

"Yeah, I did. That's right. When we were waiting to undergo the Finger Finder test, Leon told us he had no fear, and he wasn't scared."

Belle snorted."And what rubbish that was."

Fozzy laughed. "True, but the point was a good one. As we were running, all I could think of was the round's title. Do you remember?"

Belle nodded. "It was called 'The Ultimate Challenge', I remember."

Fozzy's fingers clicked. "Bang on. It did not seem … right. Something bugged me as soon as I saw it.

"The Ultimate Challenge? Surely that comes at the end, not the start. Right?"

The other three agreed. Fozzy began chattering. "Why would they put in the most formidable challenge at the start? It makes no sense. There is no way OverPower gets easier as you go. That would go against every single video game ever created."

By now, TC, Belle and Sam were listening raptly to every word and Fozzy's mind was going at 100 miles an hour. "And then I couldn't get Leon's words out of my mind. He'd said: 'I'm going into this game with no fear. It doesn't scare me. In fact, OverPower should be frightened of me.'

"Then it came to me in a rush. Leon was right.

"With this in mind, what is the Ultimate Challenge?"

No one replied, so Fozzy answered for them.

"It is simple when you think about it. They were not challenging us. They wanted us to challenge *them*."

Sam had no idea what Fozzy meant. Belle had a blank expression, although TC was smiling broadly.

She knew.

Fozzy continued: "When the second sign told us to follow the path, OverPower told us where to go. If we'd have followed those instructions, the wolves would have caught us, and our game would be over.

"The Ultimate Challenge was to break OverPower's rules. Unfortunately, it wanted us to follow the path, so I knew we could not go that way.

"Of course, the pack was right behind us so we couldn't go back. That left one way – down here."

Sam felt shellshocked. He'd have never worked that out. "That … is brilliant. So, OverPower wanted us to be brave enough to ignore its suggestion?

Fozzy nodded. "That's right. I challenged OverPower and, when each of the team jumped off that cliff, all of you did too.

"We stood up to OverPower – and luckily, it worked. I'm sure there'll be tougher challenges ahead, but at least we know one thing now."

Sam answered for everyone. "What?"

Fozzy replied with a whisper: "That OverPower – and probably everything in this rotten game – cannot be trusted."

CHAPTER 23

Belle's mind was spinning.

She looked at Fozzy in awe, like it was the first time she'd seen him.

He was incredible.

She'd have never worked out the puzzle.

She'd trusted OverPower blindly when she should have been questioning everything.

The Ultimate Challenge? She'd barely given it a second thought but the answer had been in front of them.

Belle had wanted to run. If Fozzy hadn't jumped, the wolves would have caught her.

Instead, they'd followed him – and Fozzy had been right.

Belle and Sam spoke at the same time.

"What does 'Punishment' mean then?"

To their disappointment, Fozzy held up his hands.

"No idea. Perhaps OverPower wants to punish us for defying it?"

"Hmmm," said Belle, unconvinced.

Throughout its history, OverPower did not punish contestants.

It challenged them and made them think outside the box.

The game was tricky, for sure, but never mean. Nope, it didn't sit right.

No one replied and Fozzy pulled a face.

"Look, it was just a guess.

"The answer to the last round didn't come to me straight away either.

"Let's face it. OverPower is unpredictable. There's

a good chance that 'Punishment' is not even a clue this time around."

Sam pursed his lips.

"Punishment is an anagram of nine thumps if that helps, although I'm not sure it does," he suggested.

Fozzy quickly rearranged the letters in his head: "You're right! Never had you down as an anagram king, Samuel?

"Nine thumps, eh? Not sure how that could help us either but good to know."

Belle tilted her head, no longer listening to either of them.

She stared upwards. The slither of the sky remained bright blue.

The wolves had disappeared.

But there was something else.

"What's that?" asked Sam, hearing the strange noise.

Belle closed her eyes, trying to maximise her ability to listen.

There was a tiny rumble far away. It was hard to pinpoint.

Yet it was there nonetheless.

TC was tugging Belle's arm again.

She pulled away, trying to concentrate.

They all listened intently.

The rumble was getting louder.

Belle felt TC's hand on her arm again. The grip was tighter this time, more insistent.

Belle whispered: "TC, stop it. We're all trying to listen. You should be too."

Yet it did not work.

TC did not let go. Instead, she tugged Belle's arm repeatedly.

Belle rarely got angry, but this was not the time for games.

She twirled around to face TC, fully intending to tell her to stop this nonsense.

Their eyes met.

And TC pointed in the canyon direction that none of them had trodden.

Belle saw a glimmer on the floor.

She knelt and gently touched the surface.

It was wet.

Had it been before?

The bottom of the ravine was a slope.

She placed a palm on to the floor and felt the water trickling.

It was travelling quickly.

The water wasn't here when they'd landed.

"It's getting louder," Fozzy exclaimed, still trying to find the source of the growing noise.

It came to Belle in a flash.

Nervous energy surged through her as she leapt to her feet.

There was no time to lose.

TC was already moving. The boys looked at the pair of them with confusion.

Sam stepped forward: "What's wrong?"

Belle began scrambling up the rocks as she answered.

"Get climbing.

"They're going to flood this whole place. Move!"

CHAPTER 24

There was little time for discussion.

No opportunity for more questions.

While they wasted time congratulating themselves, Round Two had begun.

And it had caught them out.

The noise was getting louder.

By now, TC was already three metres above the ravine's floor. Belle was not far behind, scaling a handily placed pile of boulders.

The boys raced to catch up.

The team were focused and, apart from the odd shout of encouragement, climbed without a sound.

Belle risked a look behind them – and immediately regretted it.

Water had submerged the spot where they'd been standing. Perhaps a quarter of a metre deep, foaming water raced over the floor at tremendous speed.

It was rising absurdly quickly.

She guessed The Video Game Kids would not be able to climb fast enough to escape its clutches but pushed that fear deep inside her.

They had climbed 30 metres up the cliff-face but were a long way from reaching the top.

And worse was coming their way.

The noise – merely a faint rumble moments ago – kept getting louder.

It echoed off walls in the narrow valley, making it difficult to think.

Events were unfolding at lightning speed, making it hard to understand what was happening.

Then they saw it – a wall of water heading in their

direction at mind-boggling speed.

They had seconds before it struck.

None of them would be able to hold on when the water hit them.

Then Sam spotted the answer.

"Here! Behind here. Quick!"

It was a broad ledge with a slight overhang, protected on one side by a pile of boulders.

Fozzy was next to Sam. Within a flash, he tucked into the deepest part of the overhang, out of the way.

Above them, TC moved across the wall like a spider and calmly dropped down into the safe haven.

Belle was further out. She scrambled across the boulders as the others disappeared out of sight.

Only Sam waited.

Her best friend, the person she always relied upon.

The calmest guy she knew, Sam faced the terrifying display of nature with barely a flicker of worry.

Sam offered one hand to Belle with his remaining arm wrapped around a boulder.

The wave was nearly on top of them.

She saw Sam's eyes go wide, a reaction that sparked fear deep inside her.

Sam did not get scared.

But everything was different here.

"Belle, grab it. Come on. You're there. I've got you," he grunted.

Yet half of Sam's words did not reach Belle's ears.

The water crashed into them.

Never-ending plumes of spray left the rockface slippy.

Sam and Belle could no longer hear anything.

The tidal wave was here.

Belle staggered and slipped towards Sam's position.

Water struck her from every direction. There was no way out.

She could no longer see Sam's face, and his outstretched hand was slipping out of sight.

Belle could not speak. Water filled her mouth every time she opened it.

Sam's hand had disappeared. Belle's eyes remained fixed on the spot where it had been.

Powerful waves battered her.

Water was everywhere. There was nothing else.

In desperation, she let go of the rocks and flung herself in the direction of Sam's hand but her foot slipped.

She fell forward on to the narrow rock ledge.

Her shoes scrambled against the side, looking for any form of foothold.

There was none. Belle's body dropped downwards, leaving her hanging by the fingertips.

She couldn't shout for help.

Within seconds, her arms started burning. She was so close. Sam must be nearby.

But she could not hold on.

OverPower had beaten her, she realised. She hoped the others would find a way out of this nightmare.

Her fingers stung with pain until they could hold her no more.

And then Belle fell.

CHAPTER 25

Silence filled the library.

Moments earlier, everyone celebrated their classmates had become East Street's best OverPower performers.

People hugged.

Others sang football songs in joy.

Teachers shed tears of disbelief.

Leon continued to bore people about how he had inspired the great attempt.

They giggled as the team with the worst name ever had made history.

Then came the water.

And the atmosphere changed completely.

The laughter stopped.

The tears dried up.

They'd watched the team race up the vertical rockface in mounting horror.

They witnessed TC's incredible climbing ability that none of them knew she possessed.

They watched Sam discover the perfect place to escape the danger, with Fozzy and TC soon joining him.

And they saw Belle's desperate battle to try to reach them.

OverPower was a video game.

Spectators could zoom in and out, look around 360, and rewind to their hearts' content.

They watched helplessly as an exhausted Belle staggered only a metre or two away from Sam.

She was so close.

Yet the water had swallowed her up.

Water filled the screen as the main thrust of the tidal wave struck.

The singing and cheering seemed a long time ago already.

The East Street team was down to three.

And their classmates did not rate their chances from here.

CHAPTER 26

Belle knew.

The game was over for her.

As her fingers slipped, she waited to plunge into the canyon.

Yet this did not happen.

Something had a vice-like grip on her forearm.

Sam.

"This … doesn't … end … here," he grunted through the never-ending spray.

Belle kicked frantically. Energy filled her veins. Sam was the only thing saving her – and she wanted to help but couldn't.

She looked up, and their eyes met.

"I won't let go, Belle. I've got you. Stay calm.

"Search for a foothold. Then I'll pull you up."

Belle was astonished at how relaxed Sam was.

No sign of worry. He did not seem concerned or struggling to hold her.

They were dangling off a cliff face, yet Sam acted like he ordered fast food.

Belle found comfort in such strength.

The rock face was soaked, making the surface dangerously slippery, but Belle did not need much.

All she had to do was find enough grip to support her weight – so Sam could grab both arms and hoist her onto the ledge.

Belle forced herself to dangle without moving, trusting Sam's grip entirely. Then, centimetre by centimetre, her trainers began to grip into the wet rock, looking for enough space to plant an entire foot.

Sam shouted encouragement from above.

"Breathe, Belle. I'm not letting go.

"Keep calm. Find your feet. You've got this."

Trying to prevent nerves from taking over, Belle focused on her feet.

Then her right foot partly sunk into the cliff. It was not much, but she hoped it was enough to hold her weight.

"Got it."

"You sure?"

Belle gently tested the foothold.

It held her weight – for the time being.

With the foot planted in the crevice, she pressed her other leg against the wall. It wasn't much help but provided some extra stability.

"Yep, do it."

Sam let go.

Belle kept both hands above her head and tried to cling on with her fingertips, willing the foothold to remain strong.

There was no need to worry.

A split second later, Sam returned. He got a proper grip and used both hands to pull Belle up to the ledge without fuss.

Belle crawled over Sam to find Fozzy holding Sam's feet.

"Welcome back, dude," Fozzy said casually, as if this sort of thing happened every day.

Then Belle remembered Fozzy had nearly been thrown down the school stairs yesterday, so perhaps he did understand.

It seemed a long time ago now.

Belle clambered away from the edge before TC helped her squeeze into the small overhang. The boys joined them as the water continued to crash around them.

They were safe for the moment.

There was little point in talking. It was too noisy.

Their soaked clothes dried within seconds. OverPower seemed so lifelike that it was easy to forget they were still in a video game.

After a couple of minutes, the storm began to peter out.

Soon, they could see again.

Fozzy risked a look outside.

The tidal wave had gone. The Video Game Kids could safely leave their hiding place.

He excitedly waved to the others that the danger had passed.

As they joined him, a shadow of concern fell over Fozzy's face.

"What is it, Fozzy?" Belle asked, unsure if she wanted to hear the answer.

"The canyon. It's still filling up – fast.

"We've gotta move, or we're going to drown. And that'll be the end of our game."

CHAPTER 27

Fozzy watched the increasing water levels with dismay.

Without a second thought, the group had left the safe overhang and begun to climb again.

Progress was slower now though.

Unlike their clothes, OverPower had not been kind enough to dry the rockface.

Everything was wet.

One slip in concentration, and they'd fall.

The water level was already approaching the crevice that'd saved their lives a few minutes earlier.

Fozzy, the last of the group to leave their short-lived safe haven, estimated they'd managed to climb five or six metres.

The clifftop looked a long way off.

This was a one-sided race.

At this rate, the water would easily cross the finish line first.

Yet OverPower did not work like this. It was never unbalanced.

You always had a chance.

Fozzy tried to rack his brains.

How could they get out of this?

What was he missing?

"Keep up, Fozzy," shouted Belle, the closest to him as usual.

She was right.

Fozzy needed to move.

He began searching for safe footholds, looking for the grips the others had already successfully used.

He forced himself not to look down.

Far above, TC was leading, trying to find the safest route to the top.

Fozzy could see TC far to his left.

She was waving frantically, trying to get their attention, but Fozzy was too far away to help.

Whatever was wrong with TC, there was one plain truth: they were not moving quickly enough.

The rising water level kept coming.

By now, Fozzy was on Belle's heels.

He took a moment to catch his breath and risked another look down.

Almost half of their old hiding place was already underwater.

It was coming for them.

And Fozzy would be the first to get sucked in.

A dark flash caught his eye.

Fozzy's stomach flipped.

It couldn't be. It wasn't possible.

There! Another flash.

And another.

Fozzy felt the air leave his body.

Terror does funny things.

He saw it again.

In plain view.

Only a few metres below.

Fozzy gathered his wits and yelled at the top of his voice.

**

You could hear a pin drop in the East Street School library.

Pupils and teachers watched the screen in horror as their champions tried to scale the impossible cliff.

Somehow their team still had four members.

Sam's heroics to save Belle had bought thunderous cheers from the watching crowd.

But the joy was short-lived.

The floodwaters would soon catch their champions.

No one had any suggestions. There were no bright ideas.

They could not help – even if they'd been able to.

At the back of the library, Mrs Tomlinson leaned over to Mrs Millman.

"How long have they been playing?"

"Almost 27 minutes," replied Mrs Millman, checking her watch.

Mrs Tomlinson began to bite a fingernail.

"Let's hope they make 30 minutes, eh? Wouldn't that be wonderful for the school?"

"Yes, I think…."

Mrs Millman never got the chance to reply.

Instead, Fozzy's scream filled the room.

One word. And it sent a chill down the spine of everyone watching.

"SHARK!"

CHAPTER 28

From her vantage point, TC could see Fozzy was right.

Dozens, perhaps hundreds, of dark shapes circled beneath them.

Most people TC knew were terrified of sharks, but she had always found them fascinating.

They didn't do much.

Ate. Swam. Had babies.

There was nothing complicated about being a shark.

And TC liked that simplicity.

The rising levels meant the water – and the sharks – were closing in fast.

With a deep breath, TC forced herself to concentrate on the team again.

She'd been trying to get Sam's attention, but he was not looking towards her.

The shark warning seemed to have increased everyone's pace, and Sam was now almost beside her.

Finally, he looked in her direction and TC waved wildly again.

This time it worked.

"What?" asked Sam, with a puzzled look.

TC pointed to her eyes and signalled upwards.

Sam's eyes followed.

"Look up there?" he asked.

TC gave a thumbs up.

Sam stared in the direction TC had pointed.

"What?"

He couldn't see. The curve of the rocks blocked his vision.

TC beckoned him to come closer, which he did.

Standing side by side, she pointed and his eyes followed.

He nodded.

TC smiled. She knew he'd seen it too.

She set off again, anxious to reach their goal.

Below her, Sam shouted to the others.

"Belle, Fozz! Hurry. Come quickly.

"We don't need to get to the top.

"TC has found something.

"It looks like a door – and a way out of here!"

CHAPTER 29

Belle's arms ached. Her legs felt like jelly.

Exhaustion filled her mind.

She laid flat on her back.

Moments ago, she'd reached the small platform that jutted out from the canyon walls.

Cut deep into the rock face, the stone area was wide enough for the champions to stand and walk.

Eyes closed, Belle stayed sprawled out on the floor, trying to catch her breath after the mad dash.

Nearby, she could hear Sam encouraging Fozzy, who was the only one not to reach the platform, to keep going.

"You're nearly there, Fozz Man!

"No, don't look down. Instead, concentrate on your feet and arms."

Fozzy had struggled.

Until he'd seen the sharks, Fozzy had been quite close to Belle.

But the predators' arrival seemed to strike fear into him.

Belle had stayed with him for most of the climb, but aching muscles forced her to finish the final section alone.

It was a good move, Belle knew. She would not have been able to hold on for much longer.

She could hear the grunts below as Fozzy scrambled to reach the platform.

She sat up.

Sam was lying full-length on the rock, just like when he'd saved her.

Belle felt a sudden pang of thankfulness that Sam

was with them. He was one in a million.

With an effort, she got to her feet and crept towards Sam. She peered over the side and immediately wished she hadn't.

Fozzy was close, only a couple of metres away from Sam. But that wasn't what shocked her.

Lapping at the soles of Fozzy's feet, the water continued to rise at a fearsome pace.

It would soon be with them.

And the sharks would follow soon after. They were no longer dark menacing shapes.

They were close enough for Belle to see their eyes and fins.

And teeth. Huge white teeth.

Backing away from the edge, Belle feared she did not have the strength to climb again.

She did not have the energy.

"Got him," Sam yelled.

"Pull, pull, pull," Fozzy bellowed as he scrambled up the rocks.

Belle saw the strain on Sam's face as he hauled Fozzy over the edge to safety. For the time being, at least.

That sent another shock through her.

Earlier, Sam had saved her without breaking a sweat.

He was never tired and did not complain. He didn't flag. Even illness seemed to avoid him.

Yet she watched in horror as Sam and Fozzy lay on the ground, gasping for air.

Sam did not get breathless. Nothing was a struggle for him – ever. He was one of those annoying people who could do everything.

Thoughts raced through Belle's mind.

Sam was tiring.

Fozzy was the weakest climber.

And she had nothing left to give.

Soon the water would catch them.

And the only one who could get away was TC.

Belle twirled around, looking for the team's fourth member.

She was about ten metres away at the far end of the platform.

The door.

Belle heard Sam shouting about an escape route but had not paid much attention.

Climbing had required 100 per cent of her concentration.

Using her last energy reserves, Belle moved to TC, who was paying no attention whatsoever to the others.

The outline of a door shined brightly against the dark rocks.

It stood about two metres tall, Belle guessed, with a white circle, the size of a melon, in the centre.

There was no handle or hinges.

It was part of the wall. There was no way to get fingers into the cracks and yank it open.

TC's eyes told Belle one thing: she did not know how to open it – and save them all.

The small girl threw her whole weight against it.

The door didn't budge.

Belle took a turn.

The same result.

They smashed it together.

It held firm. This wasn't working.

"Open the door," shouted Sam as he and Fozzy approached.

Martin Smith

Belle knew why Sam was speaking so bluntly.

Small waves were creeping on to the platform. Soon it would be flooded, deep enough for the sharks to move in.

"It won't budge," Belle replied.

Like the others, Sam smashed his shoulder at full power against the door.

Nothing.

Fozzy joined him and they tried together.

It made no difference.

The door would not open.

Belle stood back as the other three champions tried to push it open with all their might.

"What are we missing? There must be something. We started at the bottom and the round began…."

A memory popped in her head.

Words formed in her mind.

It was only a few minutes ago but, to Belle, it felt like a lifetime.

Belle felt coldness seeping into her feet. The water was now spilling across the ledge.

The shark's fins looked enormous. They were close, hungry and waiting.

Her heart began to beat faster.

"Surely not. Did we…."

She spoke the words aloud but did not finish the sentence.

"PUSH!"

TC, Fozzy and Sam were straining with all their might against the door, trying to prise it open with brute strength. It did not work.

"Out of the way," blurted out Belle, manners forgotten.

The others look stunned.

"Why? Do you know something?"

Belle ignored Fozzy. This was her call.

If she got it wrong, it was game over.

Without a word, Sam immediately shepherded the others away way to give her space.

By now, the freezing water had reached their ankles.

This was their last chance. Belle took a deep breath.

She banged a fist on the circle of the door.

Nothing happened. Belle repeated it. And again.

It remained closed.

"Belle, what are you doing? It's not working."

Sam put a finger to his lips to tell Fozzy to keep quiet.

Belle ignored them. She was counting the blows.

Five.

Six.

Water was lapping against her knees. The sharks would be upon them any moment.

Seven.

Still, the door held firm.

Eight.

"Belle. Help us…."

She blocked it out.

Nine.

As the last thump landed, the door swung inwards.

Their escape route was finally open.

CHAPTER 30

Belle plunged headfirst through the open door with TC close behind.

Sam didn't hesitate. He grabbed a terror-stricken Fozzy, and they crashed through the opening together with a splash.

They landed in a heap as the door slammed tight, leaving the sharks behind.

"Yes!"

"We made it!"

"Wow!"

They hugged each other with delight.

Against all the odds, they had somehow survived. Again.

The champions were standing in a dimly lit cave with a tunnel at one end where daylight peeked through.

It seemed safe – for the moment.

Sam looked at Belle in astonishment.

"How? What did you do? I don't understand."

"Yeah, me too," agreed Fozzy.

TC nodded eagerly too.

Belle smiled.

"It was you, Sam. All I had to do was remember."

Sam's cheeks went red.

He replied honestly: "I have no idea what you're talking about."

Belle smiled.

The others waited, desperate to know the answer.

She said: "OverPower is not straightforward. Fozzy showed us that – but it is not unfair either.

"They give you help. You just have to understand

potential clues and when to use them.

"Take this round. The water would have caught us. Or the sharks.

"It was like the first round when the wolves were so close to finishing our game."

"This all makes sense, but what has it got to do with me – or opening that door?" asked Sam, completely confused.

Belle scowled at Sam's impatience.

"I'm coming to that. Don't interrupt me – we don't have much time. Think about the last round. The game started without us even knowing and nearly caught us out."

Sam held up his hands as a peace offering and kept quiet.

Belle continued: "Getting to the door was tough. Apart from TC, all of us struggled with the climb. I'm not sure why."

TC began to point excitedly, probably to indicate they needed to start moving again.

Belle couldn't be sure but ignored her anyway, determined to get the story out. They needed to hear it.

"We had done so much. But the door – despite everything we tried – was immovable.

"Why would they place an immovable door in our way? What would be the point of that?

"OverPower never does anything without reason, does it? And then it clicked.

"I remembered us standing on the canyon floor after we'd all followed Fozzy with the crazy jump off the cliff.

"Fozzy, do you remember what you called Sam down there?"

From the blank look on his face, Fozzy had no idea.

"Er…."

Belle did not need an answer.

"You called him an 'anagram king' if I remember rightly."

"Yeah, he did," Sam agreed.

Belle continued: "Sam solved the puzzle before we'd even started. It was just we'd all forgotten."

Fozzy clicked his fingers excitedly. "The anagram of 'punishment' is 'nine thumps', which you did to the door to open it!"

Belle nodded. "Bingo. Nine thumps. That opened the door. We had the answer the entire time."

"Wow," said Sam, looking at Belle with respect. "You're pretty smart."

She laughed: "It wasn't me who worked it out! You did the hard work. All I had to do was remember it."

They laughed together. Sniggering turned into giggling. Then the team howled until their stomachs hurt and tears ran down their cheeks.

Sam was unsure if it was relief or excitement. Either way, it felt great.

The chuckling seemed to wash away the tension and the stress of the previous rounds.

Their clothes were dry again.

They did not feel tired anymore.

The exhaustion passed.

One by one, the chuckles faded but the smiles remained.

The Video Game Kids were still in the game.

Belle felt another tug on her arm. She tried to sound patient: "Yes, TC. What's up?"

Her teammate pointed at the inside of her elbow. TC tapped her skin once and, out of nowhere, a display panel popped up in mid-air.

The others gawped at it, mystified.

"What's that?"

"How do you do that, TC?"

Sam studied the girl's numbers carefully.

Health – 78
Stamina – 92

Belle did the same immediately, and a similar panel popped into the air.

Health – 59
Stamina – 31

"Wow. Hanging off that cliff must have hurt more than I thought."

With another tap on her arm, Belle closed her stats.

Fozzy went next.

Health – 94
Stamina – 49

"Wow, healthy but tired, Fozz?" Belle laughed.

Fozzy shrugged.

"Sounds about right. Nothing new there."

Sam felt a stab of dread. How had they got so far without realising they had a health bar?

He tapped his elbow and watched the stats come to life. His eyes went wide.

Health – 36
Stamina – 9

Now he understood why he'd been so exhausted on the climb.

Belle's hands covered her mouth.

"Oh no, Sam."

She knew.

He'd used up almost his entire energy to save her.

It was the team's first major mistake. And it might cost them.

"Why is my health so low?" Sam looked puzzled as the stats disappeared again.

"I'm not sure, but it begins to drain away from your health when your stamina runs out," suggested Fozzy.

"It's what happens in lots of video games. For example, saving Belle, climbing the cliff and then trying to force open the door – combined to destroy your stamina and started to eat through your health.

"Your stamina should rebuild if you don't run for a while. Unfortunately, health is usually a lot harder to regain."

Sam kept his chin up. "I'm fine. We can't change what's happened. I would save Belle without a second thought every time. Don't dwell on it. It is what it is."

No one replied. They did not know what to say.

Against all the odds, The Video Game Kids had survived again as a team.

But big trouble was looming.

And all they could do was go out and face it.

CHAPTER 31

Without another word, the foursome began to move towards the tunnel at the far side of the cave.

As they stepped into the mouth of the tunnel, new words magically floated in front of them.

Round Three
Divide

They vanished as quickly as they appeared.

"I don't suppose anyone knows a handy anagram of 'divide', do they?" asked Fozzy, hopefully.

"There isn't one," replied Sam confidently.

"OverPower does not repeat things. It may be a clue, but it won't be the same as the others, I'd guess," said Belle, taking the lead as they began to walk towards the light.

"The clock is ticking. Let's not waste time again. We need to work out what we've got to do this round."

Belle and TC led the way. Sam and Fozzy lagged behind, ensuring their stamina continued to recover rather than waste it.

By the time the boys had reached the entrance, the girls were standing by a nearby sign with an arrow pointing left.

The landscape was almost identical to the first round.

Lush green grass. Blue sky without a cloud in sight.

And a path was running through the middle of it. As before, unseen birds provided the soundtrack.

Sam nodded at the signpost and said what every

team member was thinking.

"Do we trust them?"

Fozzy laughed. "Yes. As Belle says, OverPower doesn't repeat itself. Instead, good video games have fresh ideas and challenges. That's what brings the gamers back. We've already challenged them once so this round will be something else."

Sam shrugged, satisfied with Fozzy's reasoning.

TC scanned the horizon constantly, willing to get moving.

Belle took charge. "Let's move. Fozzy made the right call earlier, so let's follow his advice. We can walk for now – at pace – and save running for when needed."

There were no complaints or arguments.

They walked in silence, each regularly checking their health and stamina stats.

Brief rest from the challenges had done them good – even Sam's stamina had risen to 25.

Would it be enough? Fozzy doubted it but reaching round three was still incredible.

He tried to stop excitement from overwhelming him. He had to focus.

Fozzy was sure they'd been playing for a long time.

There were no clocks or watches to confirm, but it seemed like an age.

He maintained a brisk walk with Sam, willing their stamina figures to go up.

The girls had run ahead, shouting about something in the far distance.

Sam looked at Fozzy.

"What are they saying?"

"No idea."

Everything remained still. Birds chirped merrily.

They slightly picked up the pace, eager to catch up.

Fozzy saw Sam check his stamina stat: 28.

He looked at his own. It read 70.

He was getting stronger quicker than Sam, undoubtedly due to Sam's low figure making it harder to regain strength.

In the distance, the girls had stopped. By now, it was clear what the fuss was about.

A giant tree stood next to the path.

The boys broke into a light jog and soon reached the girls, who were busy examining the tree trunk.

Fozzy whistled as they approached the old oak tree. It was so broad that none of the team – even Sam – could get their arms entirely around the trunk.

Roots snaked out in all directions before plunging deep into the ground.

Its thick branches were well out of reach, and there were no footholds to climb either.

Fozzy circled the trunk, looking intently for anything suspicious or out of the ordinary.

Nothing.

Sam spoke first: "It doesn't mean anything. It's just a tree."

Belle and Fozzy did not respond.

"It is the only thing here in any direction," replied Fozzy, inspecting the grooves of the bark. "It is important."

"I agree," chimed in Belle, "OverPower always has a meaning. Nothing happens by accident. Haven't we learnt that yet?"

They spent the next few minutes searching for possible clues with no luck.

TC and Sam – whose stamina had almost reached 50 – moved back to the path, eager to move on.

Reluctantly Fozzy and Belle joined them, frustrated they could not understand the reason for the tree.

As they stepped back on the path, the birds stopped singing.

"We need to move," said Sam, unable to hide his concern.

No one argued. Nerves tingling, they jogged in a tight group along the never-ending path.

Soon, the mysterious tree was left far behind.

Fozzy heard it first.

It was terrible.

An ominous rumble he hoped they would never hear.

It was the most dangerous sound in OverPower.

"What's that?"

Belle's voice wobbled as she spoke.

They looked at Fozzy.

His face turned white.

He spoke quietly, little more than a whisper.

"The Roller is coming."

CHAPTER 32

Screams filled the packed East Street library.

The appearance of The Roller had that effect on audiences across the world.

"No!"

"Run! Quick!"

"Get moving!"

Mrs Tomlinson could no longer watch as the tension increased. Mrs Millman checked her watch for the hundredth time that morning.

"They've already done 42 minutes. If our champions can survive another 60 seconds, it will have been an incredible achievement for our school and country," she told the class, trying to remain positive.

A few children nodded.

Every pair of eyes remained glued to the screen.

The Roller was here.

And The Video Game Kids were in its sights.

**

"GO! NOW!"

Sam shouted as The Roller appeared on the horizon. He sounded calm, despite fear rushing through his veins.

The giant brown machine resembled a huge rolling pin. It was a long way from them, but it would soon be here.

And they knew what that meant.

No one survived The Roller.

Most people got squished in the first round. Game

over.

They'd been lucky – in some ways – to get to the third round without facing it.

But their good fortune had run out.

Fozzy asked: "Where?"

Good question. You could not slip past the side of The Roller – it was too broad and three metres high.

Sam looked around, trying to think.

He shouted: "Back the way we came. They tricked us with the sign – again. We've walked right into it!"

The champions didn't debate whether OverPower had fooled them or not.

The mighty rumble of The Roller increased every second.

They ran full pelt, forgetting about stamina and health. TC and Sam were in front, with Belle and Fozzy close behind.

The Roller was already closing the gap at incredible speed.

Despite their best efforts, it had swallowed up a large chunk of the distance between them.

Upfront, Sam was already struggling.

He couldn't run for long.

There was no way out this time.

Their game would end when it caught them. And that would be sooner rather than later.

His mind was whirring over what they should do next.

It was clear they couldn't reach the safety of the tunnel entrance. If only the team had stayed there, it would have been the perfect hiding place.

Sam shook his head. The tunnel was out of reach.

The team needed clear minds. Calm was required right now.

There was only one other option.

"Head for the tree!"

TC kept running but pulled a face of astonishment.

Sam knew what TC was thinking without having to say the words aloud.

"Why? That tree won't save us."

He barked out a response: "Just do it!"

TC kept her head down and did not respond.

OverPower had put the tree there for a reason. The Video Game Kids just hadn't figured out why.

Slowly the solitary oak came into view — a giant alone in a barren land.

TC reached the tree first and began frantically searching for clues that could help them.

But Sam began to slow down – badly. He fell behind Fozzy and alongside Belle. It looked like Sam was running in treacle.

"Keep going, Burty," whispered Belle under her breath so the others couldn't hear.

Sam did not reply. His body hurt. He kept pushing his arms and legs forward, which were close to failing him.

The Roller was charging towards them at an alarming rate.

It did not stop. It did not slow. It was unbeatable.

When the trio reached the tree, it was so noisy they could barely hear each other.

Fozzy and Belle joined TC, inspecting every inch of the tree.

Sam could not stand, let alone search.

He collapsed to his knees, gasping for air, before opening the control panel on his elbow. The numbers were worse than he'd thought.

Health – 19
Stamina – 0

Sam grunted. His race, this time, was run.

The Roller would be here within two minutes, perhaps less.

He watched the others frantically scour every inch of the oak tree to find a way out.

Sam could not help.

The team would split in moments.

Fractured.

Splintered.

Divided.

His eyes flashed open.

That was it.

Divided.

Suddenly Sam knew what he had to do.

It all made sense.

He dragged himself to his feet.

The Roller would be here in a minute at the most.

He staggered towards the others.

"I've got it! I know how we can beat The Roller!"

CHAPTER 33

Belle gawped at Sam.

He was crazy. Barking mad.

"No way, I'm not letting you do that," she insisted, despite knowing it was their only hope.

"There's no time, Belle. This is the only way. Trust me," replied Sam.

Tears fell down Belle's cheeks. Fozzy and TC stood, speechless.

None of them wanted this to happen.

Yet Sam's theory was the only chance they had.

They could climb the tree – if one of the team stood alone and the others climbed on their shoulders.

The champion at the bottom would be stranded and at the mercy of The Roller, dividing the team.

If it worked, then The Video Game Kids would be a trio rather than a foursome.

Sam stressed he would hold them for as long as he possibly could.

It was now or never.

"Let's do this before we're all a lot thinner," joked Sam. No one laughed at the Star Wars reference.

"Sam, I…."

Belle began, but Sam shook his head.

"Dude, it's a game. I'll see you soon. Now climb – and make it quick."

Belle wanted to say more, but Sam's hair was already sweaty. She did as requested.

"Thanks mate," mumbled Fozzy before climbing on to his shoulders.

Sam grimaced. Usually, he would have held Fozzy

and Belle's weight without too much trouble but today was not normal.

The Roller was close.

Fozzy scrambled up the human chain. Standing on Belle's shoulders, he could almost reach the branches.

That left TC, who looked like she wanted to hug Sam but didn't know how. After a moment of hesitation, she gave a thumbs up instead.

Sam smiled weakly, feeling exhausted.

TC's weight made it almost unbearable for Sam.

His life stats must be nearly zero too, he knew. Everything was becoming dangerously slow.

The others were shouting, but The Roller was so close he could barely hear them.

Suddenly the unbearable strain on his shoulders lessened.

Above him, Belle grunted: "TC's in the tree! You did it, Sam."

Sam breathed a sigh of relief.

They might yet make it to the next round.

Moments later, the weight lightened again.

"Fozzy's up there too. You did it!"

Sam smiled. There was nothing else he could do.

Belle's weight disappeared too but then returned.

He did not see what had happened and it was too noisy to talk.

Finally, she went too. Sam did not notice. His race was over. The Roller was here.

As OverPower confidently predicted at the beginning of the round, it had divided the team.

Yet Sam Burton could have done no more.

CHAPTER 34

When TC reached the safety of the branches, she kept going upwards.

It seemed logical to move upwards to make space for Fozzy and Belle if they were lucky.

Once Fozzy was safely into the branches, TC disappeared.

In truth, she could not watch Sam die.

She knew it was only a video game, and Sam would be fine.

She'd see him in a few minutes. But it felt real.

And TC couldn't face losing a friend.

She did not want OverPower to end.

Everyday life would have to resume, but TC was in no rush to go back.

Inside the game, she felt like she could accomplish anything.

At school, she was The Girl Who Didn't Speak. She was a shadow at East Street, nothing more.

When she left, no one would remember her. She made up the numbers and would be forgotten as soon as she walked out of the school's door for the final time.

In OverPower, she was someone.

She was TC, an ace climber and part of The Video Games Kids team.

People across the globe would be watching.

And she was playing a starring role.

At the top of the tree, she was several metres above the highest part of The Roller.

It was an incredible sight, seeing an all-conquering force steamroller towards them.

Helplessness filled TC. She bit her lip and refused to think about Sam.

Far below, she could hear Fozzy trying to save Belle.

They had seconds left.

TC turned away from The Roller, willing Belle and Fozzy to survive.

As she moved, a flash of silver caught TC's eye.

She switched positions, trying to find the unexpected source of light.

There. It happened again.

TC edged to the tip of the highest branch and pulled it closer.

It was a small silver coin, which seemed to release light pulses.

TC had never seen anything like it. Should she take it? Thinking was difficult. The Roller's noise seemed to make her bones tremble.

What did she have to lose?

She snatched the coin thing and shoved it into one of her zip pockets.

The game could be over in a few moments anyway. What did it matter?

At least being at the top of the tree gave TC the best chance of surviving. Or perhaps not.

It was plain guesswork.

The oak wobbled as The Roller charged into the tree. There was a strange groaning sound before the tree started to topple, unable to withstand The Roller's fearsome power.

TC's knuckles turned white as the entire tree left the ground.

She had to jump. Yet timing was everything. If she went too early or late, she'd hit The Roller.

Split seconds would decide her game.

Despite the din, TC heard Belle scream.

Fozzy shouted something, but it was impossible to hear.

She leaned forwards and prepared herself.

And then everything went black.

**

As Fozzy had clambered into the lower branches, he'd felt TC's iron grip release.

She was surprisingly strong.

As everyone had seen earlier, he was not a great climber but his team needed him. Belle's hands were reaching up for his help.

Fozzy wrapped both legs around a sturdy-looking branch and leaned downwards at full stretch.

Fozzy grasped Belle's wrists and pulled with all his might.

"Fozzy, I can't…."

It worked to a degree, but not enough. Belle didn't have the strength to climb up to him.

She got halfway and then fell back down on to Sam's shoulders.

Fozzy flexed his fingers, straight away preparing for another attempt.

Time was tight.

The noise was incredible.

"TC? Help," Fozzy yelled as he realised he wasn't strong enough to rescue Belle alone.

"We can save her together."

Fozzy shuffled position to make enough room for TC to join him.

"TC?"

He looked around, but TC was not there. Where was she?

"TC! Help us!"

He screamed but TC had gone.

Panic filled his brain.

His heart began to thump.

There was no other choice. He had to save Belle on his own.

Fozzy gritted his teeth.

It was up to him. He could do this.

He grasped Belle's slender wrists and pulled with all his might.

He grunted: "Scramble up, Belle. Use the trunk."

"I'm trying," she panted.

Fozzy kept pulling and, to his surprise, it was getting easier.

Belle cleverly pressed her feet against the trunk to take most of her weight. She was almost level with him.

It was working.

And then she was there.

Belle squeezed into the small space next to him with a grateful smile.

"My hero," she grinned.

He blushed. As he released the grip on Belle's arms, The Roller struck. The impact was savage.

Luckily, Fozzy's feet kept him in position.

But Belle had no time to prepare.

She screamed and toppled backwards, eyes widening as she fell out of sight.

He could not reach her. Belle had gone.

And Fozzy was next.

CHAPTER 35

It was impossible to see what was happening.

"Change camera," someone shouted at the front of the screen in the library.

For the billions of people watching, OverPower was a real treat.

You could switch to dozens of different cameras in-game, zoom in or out, and pause if something else more important came up, which it rarely did.

Yet East Street School could not see what was happening to their team, somewhere deep in the tree.

Without hesitation, The Roller ruthlessly mashed up the oak they'd been hiding in.

Sam had gone. But where were the others?

It was impossible to tell.

Silent, kids and teachers crossed their fingers and hoped The Roller had not wiped out the entire team

It did not look good.

**

The tree collapsed around him. Fozzy knew only one direction was safe. Upwards.

Tears ran down his face.

Sam and Belle were down there somewhere but he hadn't been able to save them.

The Roller was devouring their hiding place.

His only hope was to climb and leap out as soon as he reached fresh air.

It wasn't much of a plan. He was only a slip away from losing too. Perhaps less than that.

But Fozzy would at least try. It was the only

option.

Branches scratched his arms as he battled against the tide of leave and thorns. The tree was collapsing quicker than Fozzy could move.

He could see The Roller almost underneath his feet. It felt like it was sucking him in.

And then suddenly the branches ended.

It was the end of the line. The Roller was devouring the tree, and there was nowhere left to run.

Unsure if he was facing the right way, Fozzy crossed his fingers and jumped.

**

TC found herself lying on her back in the flattened grass. She gasped. The Roller was almost close enough to touch but headed away from her.

Thankfully, TC was no longer in its path.

Unless it turned direction and came back, she was safe.

She studied the huge machine. It had lost some speed. The tree was too big even for The Roller to swallow entirely, so they were moving together, giving the crusher an even scarier appearance.

TC got shakily to her feet.

Fozzy plunged out of the highest thickets and took a flying jump out of nowhere.

Somehow it was enough.

He flew over the monstrous wrecking machine and landed on his hands and knees in the muddy grass.

TC staggered towards him, yet Fozzy remained on his knees.

He did not move. Unsure what to do, TC put a

hand on his back. Fozzy did not look up. Instead, he continued staring at the ground.

"I tried, TC. Honestly, I did. One moment she was there. The next, she'd gone. It's just us left."

TC's stomach flipped. Her eyes shimmered with tears and she battled to stop them from falling.

She never allowed herself to cry.

The Roller thundered away from them. They were safe for now. Moments passed and they remained rooted to the spot.

"What's wrong with you two?"

A battered-looking Belle stood five metres away, covered in leaves and mud.

Looking like he'd seen a ghost, Fozzy stammered: "Belle? How? I … er … you fell…."

His voice trailed off.

Belle chuckled. "Luckily, I fell backwards, not forwards. Otherwise, it would have been game over.

"The tree was already collapsing, so I went one way as the rest of the tree fell the other way.

"I clung on to one of the branches and somehow hung on. And here I am."

Smiles broke out on the faces of TC and Fozzy. They hugged each other happily.

Belle laughed. "Nice to be popular. Still, we've lost Sam. And bigger tests await, I'm sure."

Fozzy's stomach lurched at the mention of Sam's name.

"Yeah, poor Sam. What a guy."

Belle put a hand on both their shoulders.

"He is. He gave up his game so we could go on.

"Now, let's do the impossible. Let's complete OverPower for Sam."

CHAPTER 36

"YES!" Fozzy roared in response.

TC nodded eagerly too.

Belle smiled at their reaction.

She looked up and down the road.

"The Roller came from this direction," she pointed with the remains of the destroyed oak tree behind them.

"That means OverPower doesn't want us heading this way. Come on."

It made sense.

And two minutes later, confirmation arrived.

The words magically appeared in front of them without warning.

Round Four
Believe

"Hmmm," Fozzy murmured. "It's as vague as the others. The clue is there. This is no different."

Belle shrugged.

"We'll work it out. Let's keep moving."

The relaxing sounds from unseen birds returned. But, happily, The Roller's terrifying rumble had disappeared.

They walked briskly, although Belle was soon out of breath.

As they moved, they checked their health stats. Unfortunately, the readings were not good.

TC
Health – 22

Stamina – 56

Fozzy
Health – 16
Stamina – 7

Belle
Health – 7
Stamina – 4

"I wish we'd never found those health panels," grumbled Belle, closing her stats with a finger flick.

Fozzy replied: "This was always going to happen. OverPower is no walk in the park.

"Heck, we've got a shot here. We can do this, but we've got to realise that it will never be easy."

The girls didn't reply. There was no need.

Fozzy was right.

Having studied the competition for years, he knew better than anyone.

They could do this. OverPower had never been defeated. And they'd already lost one of the team.

But The Video Game Kids still had a chance of achieving the impossible.

In the distance, a tower loomed on the horizon.

"What's that?" asked Belle.

Fozzy stopped and whispered: "It can't be."

He rubbed his eyes and stared again.

TC and Belle looked at Fozzy, then towards the tower, and back to their friend.

He gulped: "The Pure Tower. I can't quite believe it.

"It's true. It does exist."

TC and Belle knew about the Pure Tower.

It was the end of the journey.

If you reached the tower, the game was complete.

Numerous teams claimed to have glimpsed the finishing line, but their descriptions didn't match what stood before The Video Game Kids.

The Pure Tower was honey-coloured with green rings encircling it at regular intervals.

It soared high, far taller than any building they'd ever seen.

Near the clouds, the tower transformed into a saucer-shaped platform. That was the end game, where they needed to get to, Fozzy told them.

They stared at the Pure Tower in awe.

They'd made it.

Hope blossomed inside them because, somehow, they'd found a way.

If only Sam had been here to see this.

It was incredible and he deserved to be there too.

"Er, guys?"

Belle broke the spell.

"What's that?"

She pointed behind them where large dark specks filled the sky.

Fozzy frowned.

"They look like…."

"Crows?" Belle finished the sentence for him.

Feeling uneasy, she began to move.

"Come on, listen to them!"

Belle was right. The birds' sounds had changed.

Chilling caws filled the airwaves, replacing the gentle tweets.

Countless in number, the crows blackened the sky.

And they were headed right for them.

CHAPTER 37

Thanks to Belle's keen eyesight, they had a big head start on the horde of flying terrors.

The East Street champions sprinted, but their low stamina soon reduced the pace to a painfully slow walk.

The Pure Tower loomed before them. The finishing line stood tantalisingly close.

Caws from the crows rang in their ears. The birds were now soaring above them, hungrily eyeing their prey.

"Er, what now, Belle?"

Fozzy's voice wavered with a hint of panic.

He and TC stood at the top of a gradual slope, looking downwards.

Lagging behind, Belle caught up and saw the problem – the slight rise had hidden a deep canyon, which stood between them and the Pure Tower.

That wasn't the only danger.

The snarling pack of wolves stood on the opposite cliff top, teeth bared and howling.

"Oh man, I thought we'd seen the last of those guys in round one," muttered Belle as she eyed the predators.

That seemed a long, long time ago now.

"We've escaped them once. We can do it again," replied Fozzy. "The problem is how do we get to them?"

He was right. The wolves were – at the moment – the least of their worries.

The canyon was the major obstacle. It was deep and wide. You could not see the bottom.

Could they risk jumping in as they'd done previously?

Belle could tell Fozzy did not think so. But, as they'd said earlier, OverPower rarely repeated itself.

The ravine stretched as far as the eye could see. There was no walking around it. There was no bridge.

Belle clicked her fingers.

"Wait, I've got an idea. We...."

She didn't finish the sentence.

"BELLE!" Fozzy screamed.

A seething mass of black feathers hurtled towards her from behind.

Belle ducked. She did not know where the danger was but trusted Fozzy's warning.

The crow missed Belle's head by a whisker.

Then it ploughed into TC, knocking her off her feet before taking to the skies again.

TC wasn't hurt, but the surprise attack had shocked her. More and more birds were circling. Others were coming towards them.

Keeping low to avoid the swooping attacks, Belle crawled on hands and knees over to TC.

"I've got you. Are you OK, Thalia-Claire?"

TC looked stunned that someone had used her real name. Belle smiled.

"We've been in the same class for years, TC.

"Do you think I don't know your name? How dumb do you think I am? Wait, don't answer that."

TC blushed. Belle gritted her teeth.

"Come on. We need to get to the edge. I've got an idea."

Fozzy appeared on the other side of TC and helped the small girl up by placing one of her arms around him.

Belle pressed her elbow. Her heart sank as the figures flashed up.

Health – 3
Stamina – 0

Her time was nearly up.

Fozzy and TC did not see. Neither knew how little health she had left. They were all close to being wiped out, but Belle would be the first to go.

There was only one thing she could do.

She had to give Fozzy and TC the best opportunity to complete OverPower.

Belle struggled to her feet. Then, taking a big breath in, she bellowed: "Guys. You've gotta jump. Trust me. Like they said at the start of the round: believe."

Fozzy and TC twirled around as Belle began to back away from them.

"Belle? What are you…."

Fozzy never finished the question.

"You two go on. Get over that ravine. I'll hold off those crows."

Belle did not wait for a response, her mind made up. There was no goodbye. No point in wasting time.

Hundreds of crows circled above as she walked, claws ready to pounce. One swooped. Then another. And then a seething mass of caws and feathers dived towards her.

But Belle did not a step back. Alone, she bravely walked towards the menacing horde.

As they reached her, Belle screamed a single word. "Believe!"

CHAPTER 38

Fozzy and TC tried to block out what was happening behind them to Belle.

They felt hollow, numb.

The Video Game Kids would have only two members left in a few moments. First Sam, now Belle.

They'd both given up their dreams for the team.

But how would they get over the canyon?

TC and Fozzy halted at the cliff-top edge.

Here, the wolves on the other cliff were louder. Strangely, Fozzy was glad to hear their growls – it drowned out any sounds from behind them.

"How do we do this?"

TC shrugged.

They had got further than anyone had dreamed.

The Pure Tower stood before them.

And, at the crucial time, they'd run out of ideas.

Belle had told them to jump – but was that the right call?

Fozzy was unsure.

TC did not know either.

If they hadn't already, those awful birds would soon finish Belle and then turn their attention to them.

Fozzy's mind was racing.

He left TC at the edge to retrace his steps, looking for a solution.

Fozzy risked a look at the sky.

Something was different.

Something had changed.

Vast numbers of crows had gone, already far away and leaving rapidly.

It was too late to save Belle but Fozzy could not understand why they had not attacked them too.

He froze.

His stomach twisted.

The game.

Nothing happened in OverPower without reason.

Frogton knew what he was doing.

The flock of birds had pushed them to this place for a reason. The game wanted them to come here, like when they'd leapt into the canyon or climbed the tree.

It pushed you to where the next challenge would be while continually draining your stamina and health.

Frogton wanted them here.

Why?

Fozzy twisted around.

TC remained on the cliff-top edge. She was still watching the pack of drooling wolves patrolling the far bank.

Fozzy looked to the skies again and could barely see the crows. They'd done their job.

Now new movement caught his eye, straight ahead, the direction where Belle had….

He couldn't bring himself to think about the loss of Belle or Sam.

He couldn't fail them now.

Fozzy squinted as his eyes looked far away.

His heart began to beat faster.

In the distance, the ground was disappearing at a ferocious rate.

This was it.

It was the end game. There was nowhere to run.

No going back.

A bottomless gap stood in front of them.

Razor-sharp fangs waited on the far cliff if they did get across.

And the game was collapsing behind them.

He knew what that meant. If the game collapsed around them, their games would be over too.

They were stuck. What had he missed?

What did Belle say?

Believe?

What did she mean? How would that help them?

Fozzy's face turned red.

He was lost. He did not know what to do.

**

Children bit their nails.

Some could no longer watch.

Everyone in the East Street library held their breath.

The Video Game Kids team was half its original size.

No one offered any suggestions or advice.

They did not know what their two remaining champions should do.

They simply watched.

And hoped.

**

Full of nerves, TC jigged from one foot to the other while Fozzy paced up and down.

"Come on, Fozzy, think!" she thought to herself as her friend gazed at the daunting chasm, weighing up their limited options.

After an age, he turned to face her.

TC's heart began to pound with excitement.

Fozzy had a massive smile on his face.

"I've got it."

TC took a deep breath. Fozzy always found a way.

He jabbered, unable to talk calmly: "There was this old film … and … you had to believe … there was a path … if you didn't believe … then … well … you know."

"I guess…."

His voice trailed off.

TC's excitement disappeared.

That was the plan? Really?

He planned to walk off the cliff – and hope?

Seriously?

Even if it did work, what about the wolves?

They couldn't just run off the cliff.

To Fozzy's surprise, she shook her head and blocked the way.

"What?"

His plan was crazy. TC was desperate to tell him, but something inside stopped her.

She hated this.

It had held her back all her life. Even now, she could not speak out.

In the background, more land fell away. The ground they stood on would not be there much longer.

Fozzy backed away to give himself a run-up. He rolled up his sleeves and spoke gently.

"Don't worry, TC. I know it sounds mad but I know it's true.

"I'm right. I'm going for it. Follow me. You gotta believe. I do."

And with those words, he was gone.

TC waved to stop him. This wasn't right.

But her friend had decided. There was no changing his mind.

Fozzy stumbled the first couple of paces but recovered, dodged around TC, and reached top speed.

His leap was enormous.

TC could barely believe it. Fozzy took off like an Olympic long jumper.

He soared through the air above the clutches of the dark canyon.

It seemed impossible Fozzy had leapt so high. He was almost 10 metres above TC now – and still climbing.

She gasped. This insane plan was going to work – Fozzy would make it.

And then land straight on top of the waiting wolves.

"Oh no," TC thought.

She backed up. She had to follow him.

By now, there wasn't much room left. Thirty metres away, the grass vanished as the game shrunk.

She ignored it. The challenge was ahead, not behind.

Her eyes remained on Fozzy.

He had lost some height but was still flying across the gap.

She was not too worried. Fozzy had to come down at some point, after all.

On and on he went. Fozzy had begun dropping now, yet he was nearly there.

His hands reached out to grab the far bank.

The wolves waited.

TC crossed her fingers.

Fozzy prepared to land. But he fell short.

Fozzy's outstretched fingertips grazed the rockface but not enough to get a proper hold.

TC watched in horror as Fozzy plunged into the ravine before darkness quickly devoured him.

CHAPTER 39

TC stared into the abyss where Fozzy had fallen.

There was no sign of him. Should she follow?

The jump, however, had been incredible. It wasn't normal. No way could anyone jump like that in real life.

"OverPower is a video game," TC reminded herself. "The usual rules don't apply. You can do this. Perhaps you need to believe more than Fozzy?"

She did not know the answer. But she had no other choice. Behind her, the game's landscape continued to collapse.

The wolves were still there, protecting the base of the Pure Tower from any intruders.

They could wait. TC would worry about the wolves if she somehow survived the jump.

She doubted she would. It was a long way. Fozzy had been so close, and he still hadn't made it.

What made her special?

TC gritted her teeth. Unique or not, she'd give it her best shot.

She took several deep breaths and focused on the Pure Tower.

Suddenly she felt a pulse in her trouser pocket.

What was that? Ignoring the dangers in front and behind, TC delved into her pocket and pulled out the pulsing object.

It was the silver coin from the tree – she'd forgotten all about it. It looked the same as earlier, except it now appeared to have a heartbeat.

That was impossible but TC had no other way of explaining it.

She had no time.

What was this thing? Why was it pulsating? It must do something? Could it be a bridge?

TC doubted it. Even in the crazy world of OverPower, that would surely be a non-starter.

Five metres away, the ground collapsed into nothing. Time was up.

TC could not spend any more time wondering.

In desperation, she threw the mysterious coin towards the edge, hoping it would magically turn into something that would save her.

To her dismay, nothing happened.

It landed with a faint thud on the lip of the cliff. It did not spring to life. No bridge appeared.

TC puffed out her cheeks.

The floor was shaking. Time was up. TC had to go.

She accelerated quickly, running flat-out towards the cliff edge.

TC kept an eye on the ground, looking for the silver coin.

There it was. Her left foot planted upon it when she began to leap.

Whoosh! TC soared into the air.

This wasn't an average jump. On the contrary, Fozzy's effort looked like a hop over a muddy puddle.

This was different. TC felt almost weightless, as if she was flying.

Up she climbed. The breeze on her face felt terrific.

TC loved heights – they did not scare her. It was one of the reasons she was such an accomplished climber.

She felt free. The coin, she realised with a thrill,

had done this – like a supercharged trampoline.

She sneaked a look backwards – the game was already devouring the cliff top.

Far below, the wolves were now mere dots, and TC could no longer hear their horrible snarls. She would not be landing anywhere near them.

Bright yellow filled her vision. The Pure Tower was rushing towards her.

TC focused on the tower's giant platform, halfway up.

Fozzy had said that was where the journey ended.

Even though the platform was high up, it was still below TC. Nevertheless, the silver coin had sent her almost in orbit.

It did not matter. TC discovered she could steer with a twist of the hips.

She circled. The platform appeared to be empty.

TC was losing height and finally finished the thrilling ride with a gentle landing on the large wooden platform.

TC crouched, half-expecting more wolves or crows to attack her.

It did not happen. It was quiet. After a moment, TC stood and scratched her head.

Was this it?

The platform appeared deserted. There was no information or signs.

It had a wooden floor, painted yellow, with a white archway in the middle.

TC crept warily towards the arch. Again, there was no writing on it and the silence made her nervous.

OverPower never stopped. Was another challenge waiting for her? Was this the final test?

She stepped through the arch to check the other

side.

And, as she passed through it, invisible trumpets blared.

Colourful streamers erupted out of nowhere. Balloons and confetti filled the platform.

In front of TC, giant letters appeared out of thin air:

CONGRATULATIONS
STAGE ONE
COMPLETED

TC's jaw dropped open. The Video Game Kids had done it.

CHAPTER 40

TC removed the FGI headset.

She felt like she'd been playing the game for weeks, not an hour.

She stumbled to the door and pressed her thumb against the sensor to use the release button.

As the door opened, Fozzy, Belle and Sam were waiting. They pulled the small girl into a giant bear hug.

"We did it!"

"We're famous."

"You were incredible, TC. That last jump was sensational."

After the longest hug, the East Street champions pulled apart.

Belle and Fozzy could not stop laughing. Sam looked like he could burst with happiness.

TC high-fived each of them.

They had done it against all the odds with no training or preparation.

They'd succeeded because they were a team – and they worked together.

It had been the most challenging thing they'd ever done.

A roar from in the background told TC they were not alone.

The rest of Mrs Tomlinson's class stood in the courtyard chanting: "East Street! East Street! East Street!"

Mrs Millman hugged them all tightly and said: "You were amazing, all of you. How you did it, I'll never know!"

Mrs Tomlinson agreed: "My goodness, those sharks. And don't get me started on the wolves. You were so brave. What a day."

The four champions could not get a word in.

They smiled and laughed as everyone congratulated them.

It felt like Christmas morning – only with more excitement.

Behind the teachers stood Benjamin Guffain, intently listening to someone talking to him through an earpiece.

Finally, he stepped forward, cleared his throat and spoke loudly. Everyone stopped to listen.

"The Video Game Kids. Congratulations. You have completed the first stage of OverPower."

A huge cheer went up.

Ignoring the noise, Benjy continued: "It is a magnificent achievement. However, it is only the beginning."

Silence again.

The champions looked at each other with raised eyebrows. They had completed OverPower, hadn't they?

Benjy checked his watch. "FGI headquarters tell me you have 57 minutes until the next stage begins. Take that time to prepare yourselves.

"With Thalia-Claire managing to survive, the entire team can start the next level with full health and stamina."

No one had ever completed OverPower before.

They were in new territory.

But OverPower was not finished with them.

Boos came from the crowd, but Benjy paid no attention. Instead, he looked the four champions directly in the eye.

"OverPower is the world's most formidable video game challenge.

"You didn't think it was going to be that easy, did you?"

He did not wait for a reply.

Benjy continued: "You have done the near-impossible and survived the opening round.

"Things get interesting from here.

"The real challenge starts now."

OTHER BOOKS BY MARTIN SMITH

The Football Boy Wonder

The Demon Football Manager

The Magic Football Book

The Football Spy

The Football Superstar

The Football Girl Wonder

The Football Genius

The entire Charlie Fry Series is available via Amazon in print and on Kindle today.

Also by Martin Smith:

The Football Boy Wonder Chronicles

The Pumpkin Code

The Christmas Poop Plan

ACKNOWLEDGMENTS

Thank you for reading The Video Game Kids.
For as long as I can remember, I've adored video
games. A childhood obsession – like many youngsters
– that has continued into adulthood.
As a writer, I find my best work stems from topics
that I am passionate about. I hope my love of gaming
shines through in this book. It was a complete joy to
write. There will be a sequel – more for my own
enjoyment than anything else.
Thank you again – and, if you enjoyed it, please
leave a review on Amazon. They really do make a
huge difference to authors like myself.

Numerous people gave up their time to help bring
The Video Game Kids to life:

Football novice Mark Newnham created a
fantastic cover – perfect for a new series.

Walking buddy and veteran sports journalist Alan
Poole helped shape the plot with legendary panache.

Grammar king Richard Wayte provided his usual
proofreading masterclass.

ABOUT THE AUTHOR

Martin Smith lives with wife Natalie and daughter Emily.

He is a retired journalist and spent 15 years working in the UK's regional media.

He has cystic fibrosis, diagnosed with the condition as a two-year-old, and previously wrote the bestselling Charlie Fry Series to raise awareness about the life-limiting condition.

Martin writes children's books in his spare time, mainly to keep away from the fridge and the Xbox.

Follow Martin on:

Facebook
Facebook.com/footballboywonder

Instagram
@charliefrybooks

COPYRIGHT

Printed in Great Britain
by Amazon